D1564848

THE MUSEUM HEIST

A Tale of Art and Obsession

Kameel B Nasr

The Museum Heist

Printed in the United States of America

ISBN: 978-0-99611753-4-0

For more information go to
www.themuseumheist.com

All proceeds from Curiosity Books go to the Curiosity Foundation which promotes tolerance and sustainability.

Please visit
http://www.theworldupclose.org/

To Kathe

Chapter One

The ancient Greeks were connoisseurs of bad luck. They differentiated long-term from short-term bad luck. They used separate words for temporary setback, adversity, ill fate, and twisted destiny. They classified bad luck involving a group, a state, or a family. They had progressive shades of individual misfortune. And standing apart from all those distinctions, they lived in terror of being ruined by the evil eye.

Paris—let's start by calling him Paris—has personally explored bad luck from all these perspectives. He knows that Fortuna spins her wheel and dictates human destiny. What she raises high she later cuts down, as she did with Paris. And once down, if the subject still swears loyalty to her and the gods, as Paris does, if the subject does not become vindictive or accusatory or angry, as Paris tries not to be, she will resurrect him, lifting him to an even higher plane than before his fall.

Paris never once blamed Fortuna for his catastrophe. Goddess forbid!

Taken by Paris's repentance, Fortuna grants him an island of relief: just two days out of prison, the gods arrange for him to meet someone who hears about a storage business in New Mexico that materialized from the expansive Southwestern sky, no money down, inheritors anxious to sell. He dedicates his gift to Apollo, god of the arts.

For the almost two years that Paris owns Apollo Self Storage, the gods bless him with regular patrons (as he calls them): merchants and contractors and vacation landlords. They pay in advance, and Paris has little to do but collect and record their tributes, researching and writing on the side.

On the morning of Athena's birthday, Paris rises in his modest apartment above the office of Apollo Self Storage, makes his usual yogurt-tomato-and-cucumber breakfast and then holds up his mug of mint tea to his plaster bust of Athena: *To you, Gray-Eyed Goddess.* Other scholars attribute Athena's birthday to the third day of the month of Poseidon, but, through meticulous research, Paris knows it to be the first new moon after the summer equinox. Paris bows. Shrewd Athena, you will overcome two millennia of male gods.

At eight o'clock he walks down the stairs to the utilitarian office. A storefront window looks onto the side driveway where a sign announces, *Stop and Sign In,* with an arrow pointing toward the office door. The Southwest Spanish Revival building has a ceramic-tile roof and is earth toned. Behind the office are four rows of units with overhead garage-style doors. Paris keeps the grounds neat, almost clinical, ever respecting his gift from the gods.

Inside the office, a large oak desk with an open guest register and pen on a string greets patrons. Paris, forty-two years old and unusually muscular for a classical scholar, sits in a T-shirt on the other side of the desk and opens a hardbound dissertation. He has the long dark hair of an Ithacan, restrained in a ponytail, though his ancestry is mostly French. As Rome traces its heritage to Troy, he traces his to Odysseus.

Across from the window stands a pedestal holding a statue of the naked Apollo of the Belvedere. It's next to a typical picture of a blond-haired Jesus, as if to prove that Christians pilfered the image of their savior from pagans. Another plaster statue he made of the long lost Benedetta Orpheus of Tarentum stands behind the desk next to a display area where boxes and packing tape are offered for sale. A stairway leads to Paris's apartment.

After a few patrons come and go, the sun shines through the window and highlights Apollo's plaster face. Paris, engrossed in a book, gets to a particular passage, smirks, says "How stupid," and scribbles a note in the margin. He hears a car and lifts his head to see a black Lincoln MKS pull into the driveway. A guy dressed in casual but obviously expensive clothes, size XL, walks into the office.

"How you doin'?" Paris asks.

The wide-shouldered guy doesn't respond. He signs the register as Paris eyes him. He looks like someone, but Paris can't place him. Then Paris realizes: it's not him, it's his type—a grim guy who started life as a little thug and had no other ambition but to become a big thug.

On the desk between them are keys, padlocks, small repair tools, a bowl of hard candy, as well as scholarly books and papers. Paris has a brick of halva and a box of *loukoumi* tucked in his top drawer. Posters of the Acropolis and other Greek temples surround them.

The guy writes *D. Jason* and *B-33* in the register, walks out, and returns to his car. Paris can see that he works out, most likely with free weights. Paris figures the guy can cold press four hundred. Out the window, Paris sees D. Jason drive back to the storage units.

Paris stands, shakes his head, looking out the window even after the MKS is out of sight. He paces back and forth, agitated. Something from his life experience has stirred an alert about Jason. Is it from when Paris worked in the world of forgery and fraud or from his experience among inmates? He can't put his finger on it. Perhaps D. Jason is how he himself would have turned out if a pretty, soft-spoken high school teacher hadn't made his body tingle with desire, told him that he's from the House of Odysseus, and then redirected his life to the lost world of antiquity. When he's alone, he still jumps up on a table, plucks an imaginary arrow from his quiver and thrusts it victoriously into an evil suitor, as Odysseus had done when he returned home after the Trojan War and found a cadre of suitors robbing his home and abusing his family.

Paris hustles upstairs to his apartment's bathroom, which has a window looking onto the storage lockers. He moves the shaving cream and razor off the windowsill. As he's doing so he realizes that nothing in his life is elegant. The bathroom has no aesthetics. Neither does his daily routine. He, dedicated to the lofty arts and exaggerated stories of gods and heroes, has allowed his life to descend to the level of trailer trash.

His fall was entirely due to his hubris. He was at his
height, associate professor at Princeton—the most prestigious
school for classical scholars—with numerous authoritative
articles behind him and an illustrious career in front of him.
He made a brilliant new discovery about the Eleusinian Mys-
teries, rewrote a chapter in ancient history, was revered and
respected, feared and envied. His treatise on the Pythagorean
school in southern Italy came out in mass market paperback
and became popular outside the incestuous community of
academics—something they all scorned while secretly aspiring
to emulate.

He, who had grown up in a single parent house on the
edge of the projects, stood up and laughed in their faces.

Then came prison, divorce, financial ruin, and worst of
all for a follower of ancient rites, humiliation. That crafty Fortuna turns her wheel any way she likes.

From the bathroom window he sees D. Jason's car in
front of storage unit B-33.

Jason puts on black gloves, unlocks the two large padlocks on either side of the door, then pulls up the overhead
door. He looks left and right as a mob thug would, then gazes
nonchalantly inside.

Well, Mr. Hit Man, Paris says to himself, at least bring
something in or take something out to make it look like you're
a regular guy.

Paris rushes to his sitting room, returns with binocu-
lars, and then looks at the car's license plate, which he writes
down of a scrap of paper.

Come all the way from Arizona just to look at stuff,
Paris mutters to himself. You're sent by evil Poseidon and
deserve a bronze-tipped arrow from Odysseus.

As D. Jason locks up, Paris hurries downstairs and sits
behind his desk, pretending to read. Jason returns to sign out.

"You all right on your rent?" Paris's tone is offhand.
He pulls the ledger closer to him. "Unit number?"

"B-33. Always on time."

Jason is no longer wearing gloves. His manner is as unfriendly as before.

Paris looks at the register, not really paying attention to it. "Ah, yes, Mr. Jason. Wish all patrons were like you."

"Here's for the next six months," Jason says. "Three hundred and seventy-five."

Paris writes a receipt while talking out loud. "Three hundred seventy-five dollars. Unit B-33." He hands it to Jason with a phony grin.

"There were two Jasons, actually," Paris says. "Everyone knows Jason and his Argonauts, but there was King Jason of Pherae, according to Euripides."

Standing in front of Apollo Belvedere, Jason keeps a poker face and tilts his head. "That's interesting."

Neither Jason nor Paris guesses that Fortuna has a special reason to grant Paris a storage business. Fortuna's magic comes when we least expect. We abruptly spring from *melancholia*, being engrossed in ourselves, to *ekstasis*, standing outside ourselves.

***

At six p.m. Paris closes the Apollo Self Storage office and climbs the stairs into his disordered sitting room. The furnishings are cheap and simple, typical of a guy living alone. On the walls hang classical myth posters, some with tattered edges. A bookcase overflows with books on mythology and ancient history. A plaster statue of Venus of Cyrene sits across from a statue of Artemis of Ephesus.

He's been obsessing on D. Jason.

Paris's desk is full of scattered papers, as if he is still a disorderly professor who can somehow locate every scrap. He walks to the adjacent kitchen to pour a glass of wine from a bottle of Charles Shaw Shiraz. He pokes around the fridge and brings out a piece of pita bread and a square of halloumi cheese from Cyprus, then cuts a couple of slices and sautés them. He picks up his iPod, turns to Gluck's opera *Orpheus and Eurydice*—he can't get enough of that opera—and channels it through his stereo. He returns to his computer and clicks to his ancient Greece web community. He opens a message from OedipusLex, reads it and shouts out loud, *Oh my gods, OedipusLex. You're fifty years off. Fifty years!*

He reads aloud as he types a reply. "Nobody wants to do research. They think they can know history by reading a two-hundred-page overview, 5000 BC to World War I in one slim volume. You're putting Orestes at the time of Satoris. Sure, they were in the same city and spoke in the museum, but Orestes left Macedonia fifty years before Satoris began teaching. Look it up and you'll see that you're plain wrong."

He blows off the computer and skips the opera to the third act, jacks up the volume as he sings along with what would have been a castrato voice. *"Che farò senza Euridice? Dove andrò senza il mio ben?"* What am I going to do without Eurydice? Where can I go without my love?

After the aria he phones his friend Barry.

"It's going on two years since we've been out." Barry says. "Why are you still here?"

"Pallas Athena, goddess of learning, wants me here."

"Me, I belong here. I tried to be a hot shot, but it just got me into trouble. Now I relish being normal. Five o'clock I go home and pop a beer. But you can go anywhere now, have people call you professor, take summer off."

Paris has thought about this since his parole ended, making him free to travel.

"No decent university would hire me anymore. Besides, I was already tired of teaching the same intro class year after year to freshmen who are there because it's required. Classics and history are inconvenient requirements. Students aren't interested in the past. They want practical skills, easy grades, easy money. I did too."

Paris picks up his wine and contemplatively looks up at the ceiling. "Most people continue taking requirements. Their parents require this, their boss requires that, friends, society. They never quit being freshmen. But a few try to know, and just by trying, Gaia opens up. Life stops being a requirement."

"Just what I need: a hit of your bullshit."

"I got this weird guy. Came this morning just to look inside his unit. Cash. Used gloves. Another guy came to the same unit six months ago, and six months before that, I think, but this fellow reminds me of the thugs you and I met. I got his license plate number."

"You know why I got a job? Because I promised never again to do what you want me to do."

"Just whatever information is available publicly."

"Why don't you look in his locker?"

"I too had to promise never to do that kind of thing again."

"Not to trash the place," Barry says. "Just to look inside. Make sure there's nothing hazardous. Do it by accident, like you got the wrong locker number."

"I'd have to pick the locks."

"So? Didn't you say that rules are for a lower form of life?"

The two make sounds like *yeah* and *uh* back and forth. Finally Barry says, "Give me the number. I'll see who it is then you can look inside. I never figured why you bought the storage business."

And neither did Paris.

***

When Paris steps outside, he recognizes the car that Alice, his ex-wife, drives. Alice pulls over and rolls down her window. He notices, as he always does, her pretty and kind face. She holds up a Redbox DVD.

"I'm in charge of tonight's movie."

"Party?"

"My reading group wants to see if the film is as good as the book."

She passes Paris a shopping bag of clothes from the passenger seat. "I saw these in the closet and thought you can use them. You have to go through the house. There are still areas I haven't touched."

"This weekend I'm going to Santa Fe to heckle a woman professor who claims that the Greeks were sexist, as if she can look at a magazine rack today and announce that we are not sexists."

"Maybe you'll charm her. On our first date you lectured me on the effects of the Punic Wars on women in Carthage."

"You seemed real interested."

"As if girls had any rights when they were married off at thirteen to thirty-year-old men."

"I know I live in the past, but it's impossible to live like they did because our lives are tarnished by modern thinking. We have—"

"Stop."

"Sorry."

"You writing anything else?"

"I have enough material for a book about the plants Macedonians used for medicine."

"Riveting."

"It's more exciting than 'Birds and Insects of Ancient Crete.'"

"I'll lobby my book group to take it up. I never figured out how someone who lives so much in the past justifies using modern technology."

"To understand the present. There are several ways to know who we are. One is to study another culture. That's why we're so hung up wanting to find other life in the universe."

"Stop."

"Right."

"There's another way of knowing who you are—by knowing how you react to other people. Those around us are important too."

"Ovid."

He could have had a wonderful life with her, but he blew it, and they both know that if he were given another chance, he'd blow it again. "I'm sorry, Alice."

"Everyone said I was crazy. They were right. I even waited for you, thinking that when you'd come out you'd be a new man."

As she drives away, Paris sees the sadness in her lips, freezing the unsaid interaction like an image on a Grecian urn immortalizing its cold narrative.

**

Paris walks back to his apartment, still fretting about D. Jason. Are the gods upset with him? Paris can usually point to something he did that makes them uneasy. But it isn't that. No—D. Jason is Mr. Organized Crime—although prison taught Paris that crime is rarely organized. Those who fall into crime gangs can't organize putting a pizza in an oven. Guns and brute force are their substitutes for intelligence.

From his youth and his time in prison, he's met gunmen, criminals, low-caliber types. They aren't what movies make them out to be. They have an emotional immaturity, haven't grown up, can't deal with issues, have no empathy, can't solve problems except by violence. They don't know how to talk. Perhaps much of it isn't their fault. Perhaps D. Jason had a drunken father who beat him silly.

Barry finally phones. "The car was rented to a Donald Jason from Flagstaff. The real Donald Jason had his Toyota broken into and his wallet stolen last year. He's five foot seven and weighs a hundred and fifty pounds."

"Not him."

"He returned the car at 2:00, which means that he drove right back to Flagstaff. They rented it again before closing, so it's been cleaned inside and out."

"He didn't touch anything at the storage unit except with gloves."

"How about in your office?"

"The guest register and pen. Everyone fingers them. He kept his distance, handed me a wad of bills. I still have them."

"They won't have nothing on them. And I would guess that whatever is in the storage unit hasn't been reported to the IRS."

Paris is recalling every second of D. Jason's visit, how he stood in front of his storage unit and looked around, how his fingers counted out the cash. He thanks Barry, goes to the bathroom and looks out the window toward unit B-33.

His rational self tells him not to open Jason's storage unit because if he commits another crime, especially breaking and entering, it could spell the end of a peaceful two years. Not an eventful two years, certainly. Not the kind of life a follower of ancient rites would lead, running a storage unit when he should have been proclaiming the gods and their philosophy. And he has done nothing about his dream of building a neo-Pythagorean school on a hill.

Pythagoras was the first person known to explore life's meaning. The Pythagorean community aimed for a rounded human being instead of a specialized technocrat. They promoted a world where nature, architecture, science, and philosophy merged. Paris looks around at this apartment and realizes how much he's fallen from his ideals.

He begins nibbling on pita and tzatziki.

He goes to his tool drawer and puts a few tools in his back pocket. He hesitates. His suspicion of Jason is animal, not rational. He has a sip of wine and walks downstairs. He goes outside into the warm evening air and strolls up and down the rows of storage units with his hands behind his back. The night air, the quiet, the moonless night refresh him.

He trips one of the motion-detector lights, goes inside and turns off the circuit breaker for those lights, returns outside and looks around carefully, though he knows the place blindfolded. Every so often a car passes on the road and disturbs the quiet.

He stops in front of Jason's unit and stares at it. He touches his tools and flashlight in the back pocket of his jeans, gazes up and down the row, and finally approaches and inspects the two locks with the flashlight. Forty-dollar locks. He wouldn't have a problem picking both. He had learned how to pick locks long before prison, when he was a street-wise kid. Had he not known those small tricks from his teenage years, he may have been spared the wrath of Fortuna.

Is he repeating the same pattern?

He puts his pick into the first lock, touching each of the five tumblers. Just feeling them. He walks away again and begins to return to his apartment. He stops before he reaches the office door, has a change of heart, then goes back, puts his pick into the top lock and makes each of the five tumblers click. The lock springs open.

Paris looks left and right, then walks away, rational nature taking over. He is again halfway to the office when he stops, returns, and again stands in front of B-33. He takes out his pick, hesitates, walks away, comes back, and then he picks the second lock and it too springs open. He walks away again, thinking that there might be someone watching, although he knows there isn't. He takes off the locks and releases the hasps.

The last time Paris did this, it triggered his ruin. The whole thing started as a prank to plant evidence around the Mediterranean indicating that a made-up tribe of seafaring wanderers—whom he had named the Navarites—had sailed beyond the Strait of Gibraltar two hundred years before the Phoenicians. He created and planted artifacts and then later "discovered" them. Two other items were unwittingly discovered by other archeologists.

The experts ate it up, examining the evidence and pronouncing it genuine, even making discoveries of their own to validate Paris's bogus finds. He shouldn't have been a scholar at an Ivy League. He didn't have the class they did. They knew it. He knew it. Just as Odysseus outsmarted the Trojans with his scheme of a horse, Paris jeered at the entire academic world. Everyone but one professor who was ready to unmask the scam.

As he stands in front of B-33, Paris is thinking that he must never again allow animal nature to overrule *Logos*. What a laugh, Paris declares, for Christians to turn Logos, rationality, into religion.

Paris takes out his flashlight, puts on his gloves and covers his hair with a bandana. He pulls up the overhead door and enters Jason's unit, shining a beam of light all around the small room. He sees a solitary wooden case in the center and shines his light around it. He takes a screwdriver from his back pocket and gingerly pries open the case, his flashlight pinched between his chin and shoulder. The contents are wrapped in a brown cloth tarp. He slowly takes the entire tarp out of the crate and unfolds it on the floor. When he unwinds the last fold, he sees old paintings, one next to another separated by paper. He pulls them out one by one and shines his flashlight over them.

Each work mesmerizes him. His fingers touch each piece. There's something profound about them. Paris knows little about art after A.D. 410, the year Alaric sacked Rome and pronounced the end of the Great Era. Fanatic monotheists took over, spreading their repression, replacing science and investigation with superstition and dogma, tongues of fire descending from the sky that circumvent learning and research. But the art Paris sees represent a rebirth of classicism—beautiful lines and colors which project a sublime, spiritual world. He knows he's spending too much time admiring them, flipping back and examining them again and again.

He undoes his work, returning the canvases into the tarp as they had been. He puts the tarp back in the crate and closes the lid, making sure it looks as if no one has touched it. He leaves the storage unit, looks left and right, pulls down the door and closes the locks, putting them back as he had found them.

He doesn't know any of the paintings in the crate—an old sea painting, two girls playing instruments in the 1600s. He doesn't know a Rembrandt from an El Greco. But he's entranced by them; just by touching them he feels they are great works, and he can guess that the hit man Jason is no art connoisseur.

Paris reenters his office and goes upstairs to his apartment. He puts down his flashlight and tools, and sits behind his desk. Perhaps he shouldn't have gone down there to see what was in that unit. What's it matter to him if someone is trying to build another Louvre of stolen art in New Mexico?

He promised the judge that he would never again break into any one else's property, no matter what.

Paris's judge was a piece of work. She smoked cigars in back rooms of Italian clubs—the only woman allowed in, and Irish to boot. She was rumored to have a scar halfway down her belly after someone she had sentenced stabbed her. She grabbed his hand, the story went, pulled the knife out of her belly, and turned it into his throat.

She was never known for leniency, doling out astronomical sentences just because she didn't like how a defendant addressed her. The insulted professor into whose office Paris had broken could be heard from the other end of New Jersey shouting demands that Paris should suffer. If a black kid gets two years for breaking and entering, that pompous Paris should get twenty.

All because that professor was ready to unmask Paris's fanciful tribe of sailors wandering around the Mediterranean.

Paris sits and thinks. If he suspects something illegal, he should phone the police. His life is just fine as it is, an easy job at Apollo Self Storage where he can study, and now he's ready to write articles and perhaps another commercial book.

Would pursuing Jason and whatever nefarious business he's involved in destroy his easy life?

He refreshes his computer, goes to his cupboard, pulls out a flask of retsina and pours a glass. He opens his e-mail and exclaims out loud as he types, "How stupid can you get! Do your research, PerseusToo. They didn't have plums in the Aegean until Alexander's army brought them from Mesopotamia, so how could they have gotten drunk on plum wine? But they did have hallucinogenic mushrooms, and that's what they used in their rituals. Just read what they wrote, for the gods' sake."

He sends the message, making a gesture to blow it off. It reminds him to pick up the piece of mushroom in his ashtray and take a bite followed by a swallow of retsina. He types a search for "Art Theft" and scrolls through the entries. Each site has pictures of stolen art. He flicks through many sites, downloading picture after picture, taking another sip of retsina. He flips through hundreds of stolen pieces of art taken from private collections in Switzerland, castles in Scotland, small museums in Ohio, and large museums all over the world. Chinese porcelain, paintings of plump naked women, Easter Island statues, and lots of antiques. Whatever has value gets robbed. They even steal pictures of Jesus Christ, statues of Buddha, and stained glass of saints urging us not to steal.

The pictures he sees on the screen are nice, but nothing thrills him as the paintings he had handled in Jason's unit. He takes another bite of mushroom.

Paris arrives at the art stolen from the Isabella Stewart Gardner Museum in Boston. After clicking through a couple of pages, he immediately hits the Back button and looks again, nodding. He clicks for the next picture. Rembrandt's *Storm on the Sea of Galilee.*

"That's it!"

His shout rumbles his desk. He should have noticed that the central figure in the boat was Jesus. He likes Jesus, dislikes Christians. He clicks through and sees Vermeer's *The Concert* and affirms again. He sees the Degas, Manet, and the others.

He types *boston.com* and finds a long article about the theft. The screen tells him that the pictures are valued at five hundred million dollars.

He sits stunned. He looks again—Five Hundred Million Dollars.

The screen reads, *They will probably settle on a ransom, but the thieves are holding out.* In big letters *REWARD* comes up, followed by *TEN MILLION DOLLARS.*

Paris looks at the hallucinogenic mushroom in the ashtray. He's starting to feel its effect as he gazes at the screen.

Chapter Two

In the early morning hours after St. Patrick's Day, 1990, two men disguised as policemen gained access to the Isabella Stewart Gardner Museum, a stately four-story Italian mansion in the Fenway district of Boston. They handcuffed the two guards, wrapped their mouths with duct tape, and then climbed the stairs to the ornate Dutch Masters room. Pulling out Stanley razor knives, they cut paintings inside their frames, working with relentless imprecision, not caring whether they cut straight lines, not concerned about the mess they're making. They shattered glass, damaged frames, and abused their treasures, knocking paint chips all over the floor as they roughly handled four-hundred-year-old art.

One of the thieves broke a glass case and pulled out an ancient Greek vase that had black-and-yellow geometric designs on the top and bottom and a mythological scene in the middle.

They couldn't roll the paintings because they were too thick. One was painted on wood. But they took what they could to their Datsun hatchback parked near the side door.

It is the largest robbery of any type in history. The thirteen articles stolen are valued at half a billion dollars and include Vermeer's *The Concert*, a Degas, a Manet, and three Rembrandts: *Storm on the Sea of Galilee*, *Lady and Gentleman in Black*, and *Self Portrait*.

Month after month, year after year, the police and FBI work tirelessly to solve the case. They have not dozens, not hundreds, but thousands of leads and tips, and they meticulously check each. They interrogate known and obscure criminals, crooks, and scoundrels. They check into drug connections, mafia connections, the underground art world, petty thieves, the IRA. They question and re-question the guards and all other museum employees and ex-employees—80 percent of museum robberies involve an inside connection. They raid homes and warehouses. They make it known to prisoners that whoever could give them information about the art would walk. They take DNA identification after the crime, and with advances in DNA forensics, they retest the duct tape, broken glass, and frames, recovering, processing, and attempting to trace dozens of samples.

They collaborate with state and federal agencies, Canadian Mounted Police, Scotland Yard, INTERPOL, the Columbian military, Miami Cuban exiles, the Corsican mob. They fly to Switzerland, London, Dublin, Bogotá, Toronto, Tokyo. They search the attics and basements of dead art thieves in case one of them hid the art and then took his secret to the grave. They look at just about every security camera footage in the city for that night; the Gardner itself was pressed for money and had unbelievably shoddy security, including inexperienced guards, but it did have security cameras. The robbers destroyed their tapes before leaving.

The police and FBI hand the case down from one crime investigation team to another. Each has new ideas, new contacts, new strategies, but none is able to find any useful clues except that an underworld art figure known as Tizzio either has information about the stolen art or has the art itself.

They try to track this Tizzio character through financial transactions. They try to sting him by posing as wealthy art investors, blowing hundreds of thousands of taxpayer dollars in the attempt. They try to initiate open contact for negotiations. But no one knows who or where this Tizzio is.

Impeding the police investigation are the different law enforcement agencies fighting turf wars, keeping vital information from other agencies so they can be the department that solves the high-profile case.

The museum hires its own detective service and issues a five-million-dollar reward for information. They beg and plead. They put up billboards on the freeway urging the public to come forward with information. After two decades, no one is closer to tracking down the robbers.

After the initial run into the museum, the counterfeit policemen had taken their time. Instead of the slash, grab, and run that happens in most other art or museum heists, the thieves spent an astonishing eighty-one destructive minutes inside. Usually night guards have a "dead-man switch," which they have to turn every half hour to show that all is well. For some reason the thieves didn't climb to the third floor where more treasure awaited, including Titian's priceless *Rape of Europa*.

The city of Boston cried. Year after year art lovers come together to lament the loss. The picture frames continue to hang empty on the museum's walls.

And no one is more upset than Ernesto Adler, PhD, one of the Gardner's trustees, a philanthropist, art connoisseur, and trusted art dealer. He is known to sob during board meetings whenever the subject of the robbery comes up, and he works harder than anyone to find the scoundrels and restore the art. He puts up another five million dollars of his own money, thus doubling the reward.

Dr. Adler's physician tells him to take up a hobby, take his mind off the heist, practice yoga and meditation. But Dr. Adler never stops. He mobilizes his worldwide web of contacts in the art business to monitor every questionable transaction. He keeps in constant touch with law enforcement and hires a string of investigators on his own.

And when that fails, he runs to clairvoyants and mediums. He even visits Catholic churches, kneels before Saint Anthony and drops ten dollar bills into his coffer, though he scorns religion and isn't even a Christian.

Chapter Three

On a bright early fall morning, curator Helen Muller is walking down the stairs from her South End apartment and then toward her car. She's dressed in a DKNY suit and medium heels, walking dignified like a working professional, a proper Bostonian. As she approaches her car, she looks up and sees that a few maples and oaks have started showing their autumn colors. She imagines that soon the sidewalk will fill with leaves. It will happen all of a sudden: the leaves will fall and the wind will blow them against the fences, and she will have the joy of wading ankle-high through brown leaves in her high heels.

She is about to get in the car when Paris approaches from behind. He is wearing a mediocre brown suit and has a large, thin package under his arm.

"Ms. Muller?"

Helen, naturally polite, turns and smiles at Paris as if he could be someone she knows. Their eyes meet, a natural attraction, a shy spark of mutual acceptance between man and woman. He notices that she wears her face comfortably as if it never needs attention.

"Yes. I'm Helen Muller."

"I have this for you."

He puts the package in front of her so that she must automatically take it. Paris can feel the nervousness inside his chest, but he needs to look cool and suave. He eyes Helen for another millisecond, and she eyes him back for even less time. He contemplates saying a reassuring phrase but hadn't rehearsed one.

"People who want to present their work should contact the submissions committee."

"It's not that. I'm not submitting anything. I'm not an artist. It's a present for you."

"For me? And you are, Mr...?"

"Uh...well...Paris." The name came without thought. He should have guessed that she would have asked that simple question. Why hadn't he come up with a name? Clever Odysseus would know not to use his own name, but as soon as he said *Paris*, that pseudonym sounded exactly right.

"Yes. Call me Paris."

"Mr. Paris."

He half-turns to walk away and then turns his head back to her. "Please wait for my phone call before taking any action."

"You will phone me?"

The question shows that she doesn't know what is going on. But there's no reason to say more.

He nods. "In a couple of hours." He's not only Odysseus, now he's also Paris. An unrehearsed smile escapes his face. Paris and Odysseus fought on opposite sides. Very fitting.

"A couple of hours?"

"Yes." His face returns serious. "Don't take any action until you hear from me."

He dashes off. She appears startled. She looks at the package. Looks up to see Paris walking away. She rips away one of the edges to peek inside and sees an old frame. She opens it more. Her eyes light. She rips the rest of the wrapping and sees the small Rembrandt *Self Portrait*. Instant recognition. She looks up in Paris's direction and makes a feeble gesture for him to stop, but he's already around the corner. All she does is move the empty air back and forth with her hand.

***

After studying her photo on the museum's website, Paris knows all about Helen. She has black hair fluffed and blown back, not a strand out of place. She shows a confident smile, concerned eyes people would feel comfortable confessing to, and wears simple gold earrings matching an elegant gold necklace. Nothing showy. Her neck is straight, her face long and slender. Her bio tells of a Northwestern University art history PhD and a list of jobs and publications related to art and collections. She has a solid foundation in the Italian Renaissance, a period highly represented in the Gardner Museum collection. Her employment is augmented by sabbatical research in France and Italy.

But what got Paris's attention was Helen's classic features. Although obviously not of Greek heritage, she had the tan skin and slightly elongated Mediterranean face that belonged to the House of Atreus, Agamemnon's tribe.

Paris has two minds about the controversial archeological antiquities scholar/thief Heinrich Schliemann, who unearthed Troy simply by reading Homer and claimed to have found Agamemnon's tomb—"I have looked into the face of Agamemnon," he proclaimed in a cable. Paris regards him more as a grave robber and megalomaniac than a scholar, but he admires that Schliemann chose his second wife because she had facial features from the classical world.

That's why Paris goes directly to Helen instead of contacting the FBI or the museum security person listed on the website. Helen will be his accomplice. Returning the paintings must be handled carefully. A lot is at stake.

Once he's put the package in Helen's hand, Paris wanders the streets, distracted at first, walking toward Back Bay. He goes in and out of one office building after another looking for a pay phone, which is the second step in his plan. A descendant of shrewd Odysseus would never use his own phone. There isn't a pay phone anywhere. He begins walking faster and faster, becoming almost desperate. Eventually he finds himself in Copley Place, the downtown indoor shopping mall. Near the restrooms he finds two pay phones side by side. He waits a few seconds to calm himself, closes his eyes and breathes deeply.

He pulls a scrap of paper from his pocket and dials the number. A secretary answers.

"Helen Muller, please," he requests. "My name is Paris."

Helen's anxious voice comes on quickly. "Hello."

"This is Paris."

"You have my absolute attention, Mr. Paris."

"Did you like my present?"

"The loveliest present anyone has ever given me."

Her voice puts him in a playful mood. He has to project James Bond cool, as if he handles hundred-million-dollar paintings on a regular basis.

"Probably the most expensive present."

"No doubt," she says.

"May I invite you for a discussion over lunch?"

"May I bring a colleague?"

"Of course, Ms. Muller, but you're throwing away your advantage. I would certainly be at your mercy if I had to deal with a beautiful woman alone." That's cool, thought up on the moment. It gives him confidence.

"I've been dreaming about this phone call for a long time, and now I don't know what to say."

"Dreaming about the paintings?"

"Yes, the art. That's what I mean."

"Top of the Hub Restaurant at half past twelve?"

"Certainly."

"Ask for Paris's table."

"I know what you look like."

"Oh yes. Of course you do, Ms. Muller."

"Please call me Helen. And you are Paris, as in France."

"Paris as in Helen."

Helen is silent.

"Daughter of King Priam."

More silence.

"You know…Paris carries off Helen and precipitates the Trojan War."

"Oh that Paris."

He brings up his formal voice. "My gift is a show of good faith. It's yours to keep, naturally. I mean, I guess it is actually yours to begin with. I hope you will echo that good faith and be discreet until our meeting."

"I wouldn't dream of tampering our trust. You have my word."

"Your word is more valuable than a museum of the finest art. Until lunch."

Paris hangs up and congratulates himself for being cool. He takes a moment to put on his detached business face. He pulls out another scrap of paper, inserts two more quarters and dials.

The hostess answers. "Top of the Hub."

"I'd like to make a lunch reservation for three at 12:30."

"Let me look at the availability. I'm sorry, sir, we have a private party until 12:45 and we will need another fifteen minutes. Can you make it one o'clock?"

"Nothing at 12:30?"

"I'm sorry, sir."

"Can't you squeeze us in somewhere?"

"I'm afraid not."

"OK…one o'clock…I guess."

"And the name?"

"Paris. Party of Paris."

"This afternoon at one. Thank you."

Paris hangs up impotently. He fiddles in his pocket for the first piece of paper, puts more coins in the telephone and dials. He clears his throat. Remember, be cool.

"May I speak again to Ms. Muller?"

When she comes on the line, he says, "Can we make the appointment at one? We have to wait for a table. I mean, they're all booked. I just thought that I should phone so that we don't stand around waiting with our hands in our pockets while they clean up."

Not too cool.

***

Paris's casual walk from Copley Square leads him to the Public Garden where people are strolling around looking at the fall colors. He too looks at the leaves turning shades of yellow and red and delights in the scene. The roses are blooming, the flower beds are radiant.

The park is in its glory, the sky open and bright. Weeping willows and maples and oaks line the walkways. From the columned bridge he sees people riding the swan boats around the pond. He walks under an enormous beech tree and passes the Robert McCloskey bronze statues of Mr. and Mrs. Mallard and her ducklings. Japanese tourists are taking pictures of the pub Cheers across the street. Lovers are strolling arm in arm. Buskers are strumming their guitars. Paris hasn't been this happy in years.

He strolls down fashionable Newbury Street, looking at shop windows, a smile on his face, his hands behind his back. Well-dressed women walk past him with fancy bags from expensive stores. He passes boutiques, antique stores, restaurants, cafes, a cigar salon. He delights in everything he sees. He notices several art galleries featuring a range from antiquity to ultra modern.

He stops in front of one art gallery, which has a large painting of Dido and Aeneas displayed in the window. Paris studies the painting and then walks inside.

The gallery is as bright and commercial as its art—idyllic landscapes on the walls and a couple of modern sculptures in the center, each piece illuminated by a spotlight. A sales woman seated behind a desk acknowledges Paris's entrance. He walks up to her.

"That painting in the window—" Paris begins.

"*Dido's Last Dinner.*"

"Yes, that one. It's wrong."

The woman looks at him, gives him a salesperson smile.

"I mean, most things are right. But it has Dido offering grapes to Aeneas."

"Yes..."

"Well, it's wrong; don't you see? Aeneas left in the spring. You couldn't have grapes in spring. People today don't know this because we walk into a supermarket and get fruit at whatever season, but back then, anyone would have known that in spring you couldn't have grapes."

"A good point, sir. I'd like to tell the artist, but he's been dead half a century."

"Still, it's important to get things right."

She deigns another salesperson smile, slight eyebrow raising.

If people are wrong about basic historical facts, they need to be called on it, that's all.

Having executed his mission, he too gives one of those nonsmile smiles and exits.

***

Paris can't get enough of the skyscraper view from his window table at the Top of the Hub restaurant, looking down at central Boston and out to the blue waters of its harbor.

The ancients built temples on high mountains, even though those areas were hard to reach and harder to haul up lumber and stone to build. The monotheists copied the idea, building spires and minarets reaching to the sky.

As Paris looks out the window, it hits him that a modern temple on a hill has a new meaning: it belongs on top of a building overlooking the city, a grand city that men and women built, brick by brick, timber by timber. In an *ah-ha* moment, he realizes that the Pythagorean school he's been dreaming about is a Temple of the Muses for uniting science and philosophy and art. A museum is a place to practice the Socratic method of interrogation.

This is where he should build his neo-Pythagorean school, right in the middle of the city. This is what Isabella Stewart Gardner did with her money—construct a museum for the world to enjoy. By the intercession of Fate, Isabella is passing the torch to Paris. He must bring pure philosophy without commercialism. Pythagoras was the first person to use the term *philosopher*, lover of wisdom.

He is so engrossed in his idea of a museum or school linking the ancient and modern worlds that he doesn't notice the restaurant hostess leading Helen and her colleague until they are standing around him. He jumps to his feet. He must not show nervousness. After looking into Helen's kind and happy face, he too becomes happy. They stand two feet apart, smile at each other while shaking hands, each observing, taking in as much information as possible during the brief encounter.

"Mr. Paris, I'd like to introduce Imogen Bennington, our director."

Imogen comes forward with extended hand. As he extends his hand, he notices the sleeves of his new charcoal jacket are slightly too short, and it's tight around the shoulders. Uncool.

Imogen and Paris say "A pleasure" to each other. Both women are dressed professionally, trim and sensible museum director and curator. Paris recognizes Imogen from her photo on the website. He makes a gallant bow as he presents her seat. She is not at all a soft person like Helen. Imogen was hired before the heist to take the museum to a new level. Her specialty, Paris deduces, is fundraising, not art.

He has researched the Gardner museum and committed to memory all those who work there. He knows its budget, history, capital campaigns, mission. In the last two days he's read so much about Isabella, the founder, that she's become a friend.

Helen takes a chair near the window opposite Paris, and Imogen sits between her and Paris.

"Would you like a drink to start?" Paris says.

They politely decline.

"We have a thousand questions," Imogen says.

Why rush? Why get right to business? He urges them to look at the menu. He sees Helen looking half at her menu and half at him.

A busboy puts a basket of bread in the center of their table.

"How, where, did you find that Rembrandt engraving?" Imogen asks.

"The waiter advises salmon," Paris says, taking a serious interest in the cuisine. "But then again the ravioli looks good."

"I'll take your advice on the ravioli," Imogen says, focusing on Paris.

"I'll try the grilled salmon," Helen says, equally uninterested in reading the menu. Paris notices her sturdy working hands, a true daughter of the House of Atreus.

The waiter approaches, asks for drink orders. Paris says they're ready to order lunch.

"Ravioli for this fine lady and salmon for the two of us."

"Excellent choices. Would you like watercress-and-basil salad or lobster bisque to start?"

They all say salad.

"A glass of Merlot, please," Helen adds.

"Perhaps the Hamacher Pinot Noir would go better with salmon," Paris says.

"Of course. Please make it the pinot noir."

"The same for me," Paris says. Very cool. She has no idea that he had asked the waiter for a complementary wine before they arrived. The waiter gives Paris a secret wink.

Imogen asks for a Coke.

Keep being a gentleman, he says to himself, but a quaint mischievousness lurks inside his chest. He addresses Helen. "Have you been in the art business long?"

"All my life. And you? How long have you been in the art business?"

"Art—a long time, but a different type of art. Business—perhaps I'll start getting into it now."

"What is your favorite type of art?" Imogen asks.

"I was enchanted by the small Rembrandt I gave Helen."

"Then we share tastes," Helen says.

"It makes a difference if the art is true or fake," Paris says.

"Naturally," Imogen says.

"How long does it take you to authenticate a piece?"

Imogen answers, "If it's a painting we once owned, we can tell right away."

"I knew the second I opened your package," Helen says.

"But you did tests?"

"To confirm what we already knew," Imogen says. "Would you like to check the authenticity of other paintings?"

Authenticity. She says it as if you can prove such a thing. Any historian knows that nothing is real or provable. It shouldn't be. Doubt is the basis of philosophy. Paris, an expert on fakes, knows that even the most skilled can be fooled. Forgers have sold fake Rembrandts to museums.

"Do you have the others?" Helen says.

"I know where they are. Your website had photos of the nine most valuable works, but thirteen were taken."

Imogen takes an envelope of pictures from her purse and hands it to Paris.

A waiter puts a drink in front of each person.

"Take a look," Imogen says.

Paris opens the envelope and looks at each picture. He looks at one after another and says, "Yes, that's there...and that too..."

He stops at a photo of a Greek vase. His cheery demeanor switches to somber. "What's this? I've never seen it." He studies the photo for a long period while the ladies remain silent. He's stunned. "It looks like it's from the island of Samos," he says.

"That's right."

"Pythagoras's birthplace."

Paris brings the photo close to his face and examines it in detail. "Iphigenia on her way to Aulis," he says, interpreting the scene depicted in the middle of the vase. He looks up. "She thinks she's going to offer the sacrifice without knowing that she's going to *be* the sacrifice."

Paris sees a faded inscription below the scene. He reads it out loud in Greek to the two women. He notices them exchanging the type of glances people use when they are commiserating being with an unusual person. He knows the look.

"Calchas the seer tries to appease Artemis but is taking revenge on Agamemnon by forcing him to kill his daughter. And here's the face of Aeschylus the playwright next to Agamemnon's wife Clytemnestra. She's wearing a chiton fastened on her left shoulder. Interesting. Very interesting. The eve of the expedition to Troy, all because Paris had taken Helen."

The waiter brings their salads and sets one in front of each person.

Paris says to Helen, "He didn't kidnap her, you know. She went willingly, according to Sappho."

"A modern woman."

"In the ancient world, the main reason for war was to procure women. Men could live with depravity—many are happier in depravity—but they can't live without women. Helen represents women."

"The vase is about eighteen inches high," Imogen says.

Her blunt voice brings him back to the present. "This is the only piece I don't have. Where did it come from?"

"It's always been in the collection," Imogen explains. Her face is hard. "You seem to know a lot about it."

"I study this thing, you know, classics. May I keep the photo?"

"It's a paltry exchange for your gift," Helen says.

"I'd like to see the vase. I wonder why it's not with the group that I found. Do you have a copy?"

"No," Imogen says.

Helen corrects her, "Actually, we do."

"We do?"

"I don't think anyone else knows, but I saw a copy of it in our warehouse."

"We were hoping you would have the original," Imogen says to Paris, "but if you have the others, the Rembrandts, Vermeer, Manet, and Degas—those are the most important. What shape are they in?"

"They're ripped out of their frames. But I guess you know that. Otherwise, they've been in a dry place where it doesn't get too cold or hot."

"I'm so relieved," Helen says, and her face relaxes as she expresses it.

"They're too well known to be sold," Imogen says. "No one can do anything with them except return them."

"Oh, don't get me wrong. I'm not here to bargain for more money. Heavens no. Let's leave things as they are—ten million. Wasn't that the sum?"

They nod.

Imogen asks, "How did you get hold of them?"

"You haven't touched your salad," he says, making a gallant expansive gesture.

Imogen doesn't pick up her fork. "You know who did it?"

He and Helen continue eating their salads while Imogen stares at Paris.

"I can help find him," he says. "I think he can pay back your reward, so it would be a double win."

"How do you know the thief is rich? How do you know he's a he?" Imogen asks.

The waiter removes the salad dishes, puts an entrée in front of each person, and wishes them bon appétit. Paris gestures for everyone to start eating as he picks up his fork and takes a bite. The others do the same.

"A bit dry; don't you think?" he asks Helen. While studying at Cambridge, England, he met aristocracy and discovered that disparaging remarks are a sign of being upper crust.

"Mine is just right," she answers.

Paris says, "I thought we'd both be happier if our new relationship is clear and legal." Paris takes a legal brief from the chair next to him and puts it beside his plate. "I asked a lawyer to put it into legalese. You know, lawyers are actually the world's oldest profession. They turn up in writings from Samaria forty-eight hundred years ago. Orestes turned to the courts after he killed his mother, and you can bet that he had the best lawyer because he got off, and the Furies suddenly made an about-face and became nice ladies."

The women gaze at Paris with that same bewilderment.

"Athena told Orestes to seek justice under Athenian law. She arranged for Apollo to speak in front of the twelve-man jury. What better lawyer can you get than Athena? I've always wondered why Socrates didn't get a good lawyer. Or Jesus Christ, for that matter."

"When do we get the paintings?" Imogen asks.

"I need a few days to bring them here. First of all, I don't want my identity known." He turns the page and points. "This clause says that if you reveal my identity publicly, you're obliged to double my reward, another ten million. It's better that you don't know my name."

"I understand," Imogen says. "You'll remain Mr. Paris. We assume it's not your real name."

"If you don't have justice," he says, "the ghost of the unavenged victim floats around and fouls up the living."

He takes another bite and then points to another paragraph. "The next part insists on silence until we find the thief. We're in a delicate position. Any rumor that the art has been returned may harm our chances of catching him."

"I imagine that it would also be dangerous for you," Helen says.

"What's bad for me would be bad for the museum since we become partners to catch the thief so you can reclaim your ten million dollars from him."

Paris hands Helen the document, but she isn't focused enough to read it.

She says, "We have five million ready. We have to talk to our devoted trustee Dr. Adler who promised the additional five million."

"Dr. Adler?"

"Ernesto Adler. Do you know him?"

"Everyone in classics knows him. He's an expert on

Greek art."

"That's right. He took our loss personally."

Hearing Adler's name stuns him as much as seeing that photo. Why hadn't he looked at the names of the museum's trustees? He asks, "Did he procure that Samos vase?"

"As I told you, it's been in the collection since Isabella Gardner brought it from Europe," Helen says.

"But he must have had a special interest in that vase, I mean, seeing that it belongs to the classical world."

Imogen thinks a minute. "I believe he mentioned it a couple of times before the robbery; thought we should exchange it for another better known piece."

Paris is riveted on each word. He looks down at the picture of the vase.

"Exchange it," he repeats. "A vase from Pythagoras's hometown."

"Why do you have a special interest in that vase?" she asks,

He realizes that as soon as Dr. Adler's name popped up he again stopped being cool.

"It's still a missing piece, the only item the thief has." He tries to say it casually, but it's not coming out suave.

"I'll have our lawyer look over the document," Imogen says. "Shall we meet again tomorrow morning to sign?"

"Give me the address of your attorney, and we'll meet in his office at ten. I have a plane to catch right after that meeting. After I clear up some personal things, I'll bring the art secretly in four days. Tell me tomorrow where you want them delivered—not to the museum, obviously."

"Deal," Imogen says. "Tomorrow at ten."

Helen asks, "By the way, have you been to our museum?"

"When I landed here yesterday I dashed over as fast as an arrow from Artemis's bow."

Imogen reaches in her purse and hands him a brochure. "I give this to prospective contributors."

Helen says, "Since you're not from Boston, can I give

you a tour on your return?"

Paris nods robustly and proposes a toast. "To art."

Chapter Four

Lieutenant Lowell is lying on his back in plaid flannel pajamas in the drowsy stage before waking. Easy-listening plays softly on his nightstand radio. The phone jars him awake. The commissioner, on the other end of the line, is an early riser and expects the same of everyone else.

Lowell shoots up and switches off the radio. He hears his Irish setter running upstairs, the ringing telephone signaling time to rouse the house.

"What do you know about art?" the commissioner asks.

Lieutenant Lowell is no art connoisseur. He can't even recall meeting an art connoisseur. Sure, his wife drags him to museums when they travel, and he even enjoys walking around with his hands behind his back looking at the pretty pictures.

Lowell holds his enriched midlife belly. "My daughter took art in grammar school. Came home with paint on her new clothes, which made my wife give the teacher a cold stare at a PTA meeting. That was twenty years ago, and she still remembers it."

He hears the dog using his paws to twist the door handle and barge in. Lowell grimaces.

"Art is about money," the commissioner says. "Businessmen invest in expensive paintings, keep them in a vault during periods of inflation, then sell them at a profit. Big companies hire experts to buy valuable art as part of the company's investment portfolio. They list their holdings: two Picassos and three Rembrandts, along with shares of IBM and Citigroup."

Even Lowell knows that Rembrandts and Picassos sell for big bucks. And Lowell knows that the commissioner's knowledge of art isn't much more significant than his, even though the commissioner has to regularly attend high-snob events. Lowell, a reasonable man, can never understand why one picture is proclaimed great and another mediocre. You can pick up one at a flea market for ten bucks while another sells at auction for more than the net worth of a Third World country.

"What's your sudden interest in large, naked ladies?"

Lowell's wife pulls the covers over her head. The setter is prancing around the bed, slobbering, licking everything he can. His daughter wanted them to keep the dog when she moved out. Lowell started to object, but his daughter hit him with a tirade of how embarrassed she is around him, and he shut up.

"You remember the Gardner Museum heist?"

"We had lots of people on that case."

Lowell sits up on the side of the bed, his feet fighting off the dog and searching for the slippers his daughter had given him for his birthday.

"Too many people to name. Everyone wanted to be in on the case, elbowing other departments out of the way. The feds took charge right away. They wouldn't leave it to us and then they blamed us for their own screwups!"

Lowell isn't surprised by the accusation in his voice. Police are the most territorial creatures.

"The director of the museum phoned and said that the art seems to have suddenly turned up. You're assigned to deal with it. The guy who found the paintings doesn't want his identity known so the thieves won't be able to track him down. At least that's what he says. So don't find out who he is…but find out who he is. He wants to cooperate with law enforcement to find the thieves, so he says."

"What am I supposed to do with the paintings?"

"The museum people will handle that. They'll test if they're real and dole out the reward. I don't want the same people who have been investigating the crime so far to have anything to do with this. I want a totally fresh face."

Lowell thinks himself an intelligent man. He subscribes to medical journals and tries to keep abreast of new discoveries in internal medicine. He also thinks that he is a likeable man, a warm-hearted man radiating world-class humor, a man who appreciates human foibles, who can be counted on to put failure and frustration in perspective.

When medical schools denied him, he studied human organs on his own. Now he looks at facial complexion, eye color, and finger nail texture to determine the health of liver and colon, pancreas and spleen.

He has been trying to devise a method of identifying criminals through the molecules the body emits. He knows that each individual has a specific imprint of digestive odors which pass through their breath. If a person passes gas in an enclosed space, which people do when they're under stress—and those committing a crime are under enormous stress—that molecular imprint is distinct. Lowell knows that under stress, the digestive tract shuts down to allow blood, adrenaline, and insulin to flood the heart, brain, and limbs. The body releases anything extra, mainly through breath. Humans can distinguish between at least a trillion smells. Criminals can hide fingerprints, Lowell concludes, but there's no way to perfume out the molecules coming out their mouth or rectum. If a crime is committed indoors, all investigators need do is blow up a balloon from the air inside the room and take it to a lab, where the sample can be split into parts per million of various molecules. Right away the lab would identify anyone present at the scene. Other than not breathing, there's no way for a criminal to avoid detection as there is with DNA or fingerprints.

He presents his idea to forensic experts at every opportunity. People listen, but no one returns his phone calls.

"My face was fresh forty years ago," Lowell tells the commissioner, squeezing his size-twelve feet into the size-eleven slippers.

His wife remains curled up on the edge of the bed as if trying not to let Lowell's conversation and the dog's howling wake her. Lowell stands.

"You know what will happen if we screw up again?" the commissioner says. "They'll put us in front of a firing squad but they won't be kind to us and use bullets. They'll have cameras and they'll be laughing at us."

The setter is jumping all over Lowell. He has to take him out, but first Lowell has to pee and record both its yellowness and the intensity of his stream on a one-to-ten scale.

The commissioner says, "We don't want anyone to know that we might have the paintings back. Don't tell anybody that you're on the case except the museum people. Clear? They were uncomfortable about talking to me because we messed up so many times before."

"But none of it was our fault."

"That's what they've been hearing from everybody: it's not *our* fault. I had to reassure them over and over that this time it would be different. I don't want anyone on the force to know anything about this, so deal directly with me."

Lowell thinks that if the police had his smell-machine invention, someone could have grabbed a balloon of air right after the Gardner heist, diffracted it in the lab into parts per million of various molecules and identified the robbers. Someone will eventually see the merit in his idea, and law enforcement agencies will be trampling over each other to be the first to use it.

"This could be a heartburn case," Lowell predicts. "Stress causes the cardiac sphincter to go into a tizzy, letting gastric acids up the esophagus."

The commissioner says, "Go see the museum director right away. The guy with the paintings apparently has information. It's a good bet he was in on the heist. Maybe he'll finally lead us to Tizzio."

"The pancreas can't produce enough sodium bicarbonate to reduce digestive pH. A dangerous situation."

***

Paris is proud that his meeting with Imogen and Helen went off better than planned. Helen made him feel comfortable, allowed him to play cool, except when he saw the photo of the vase from Samos and almost jumped backward. Very strange, that vase. The two ladies obviously noticed his strong reaction to it, and to Dr. Adler.

They will be bestowing upon him a huge gift—thank you, Fortuna—and he must use it wisely, invest his bequest so it expands and has a bigger impact. Now he will have the ability to disseminate knowledge of our past in order to have a more sophisticated future. Is that his hubris resurfacing?

He knows that he must not be smug or betray the gods through arrogance and selfishness, but he can't wipe the Cheshire cat smile from his mouth as he strolls, one hand in his pocket and the other carrying brochures and newspapers under his arm, through the streets of Back Bay. The Fates are giving him another crack at life. Ten million dollars. He is not interested in more comfort, but he must put the artless, loveless apartment on top of Apollo Self Storage behind him. He knows that he'll always be a minimalist—he doesn't need much to be satisfied—but a simple life does not need to be shabby.

He passes Cabot and Company Real Estate, which features expensive downtown properties in its window. He hears Athena edging him forward. Hadn't Fortuna called him to Boston? The prices are sky-high. He hasn't been in a big city for years and doesn't recognize modern prices, but he can easily spend two million out of ten for his museum. He walks down the street contemplating a neo-Pythagorean Temple of the Muses on top of a building.

Throughout human history many people helped create a better world. Pythagoras certainly, but since discovering Isabella Gardner, he knows that she was another.

Isabella was the first woman to establish a museum. After the death of her two-year-old son, she slid into depression. Her husband took her to Italy, and she fell in love with Renaissance art, beginning her life's ambition of spreading beauty. If art could cure her sorrow, it could heal others as well. She made several trips to Europe, buying from reputable dealers. Forgeries had been a major problem in the art world since art began having a marketable value in the nineteenth century. Paris focuses on the couple of times she and her husband bought expensive art that turned out to be forgery. Artists who couldn't make a go of it—it's a hit-or-miss business—turned to the lucrative art of forgery. Could it be that more pieces she bought for her museum were fakes but stayed in the collection?

Paris takes out the picture of the missing vase from Samos and looks at it again. Maybe it's his lack of fashion consciousness that prevents him from remembering the clothes of each era and each town during antiquity. Clytemnestra wearing a chiton. Very strange for a vase from Samos. He has to find out more. Why did the robbers go to the trouble of taking it along with a bunch of flat paintings? Who has it now?

***

Next morning, first day of the festival of Demeter, he is at attorney Rothman's office, arriving before Helen and Imogen, and wearing the same uncool suit. When the ladies walk into the reception area, Paris and Helen have another eyeball to eyeball. Paris is bubbling with expectation, and it's rubbing off on Helen. Even stern Imogen looks happy. The office secretary ushers them into the attorney's office, and they sit around his desk. Rothman has a microphone set up on the center of his desk.

During their introductory handshake, Paris pegs Rothman as a no-nonsense professional. The attorney points to a video camera in the corner, tells everyone that he's taping the meeting, and gets right down to business. He says that unlike dozens before, Paris seems able to deliver the art.

"When we sign this agreement," he says to Paris, "You are obliged to bring the missing objects to the address on this sheet within one week. It's a warehouse the museum owns. In exchange you will receive ten million dollars which will be dispersed within forty-eight hours, unless we prove the paintings are not authentic. If they're not authentic, then you'll get them back."

Paris looks at Helen who gives him a reassuring nod.

"For legal reasons," Rothman continues in his lawyer's tone, "I have not included any reference to you helping to apprehend the thief, but we agree to invite Lieutenant Lowell of the Boston Police as soon as you return the paintings. He will be handling the case, and you'll turn over your information to him."

"I'd like to stress the need to keep my identity secret, including from the police."

"We've gone to great lengths to make sure that the three of us plus Lowell are the only ones who know you," Imogen says.

"None of us knows your real name," Helen says.

"I'm happy to be Paris."

"I'm happy to be Helen."

"And Dr. Adler?" Paris says. "I don't want him to know who I am."

He sees Helen and Imogen stop for a beat.

"Why bring him up?" Imogen asks.

Paris sees distrust on her face.

"I know Dr. Adler is contributing five million of his own money and has to know that the paintings are being returned, but I don't want him to know me. My identity must remain secret. I know the type of thieves we're talking about; they're ruthless."

He's thinking that Adler would not know him by sight but by his reputation of creating the Navarite hoax.

Helen says, "There's no reason Dr. Adler or anyone but us and Lieutenant Lowell should know you or meet you. The lieutenant is new to the case, so there won't be any old baggage. It will be an entirely new start to solving the mystery."

"And naturally, we don't want people to know that the art has been returned because it will hinder us from catching the thief."

They all voice agreement.

"Finally," he says to Rothman, "When I come back I

will have a list of how I would like the checks and wire transfers issued. Rather than one big check, I'd like to divide them and put them in different accounts in different cities to minimize the paper trail. I want the deposits to look like equity from real estate transactions."

"Good idea," Rothman says. "I'll issue the checks and transfers through my office so they will return to my office. We have to tell Dr. Adler that the art is being returned so he can ready his half of the reward. We won't say anything else until the police finish their investigation."

Agreement all around.

Rothman adds, "Mr. Paris, as we've called you in the document, have you read the contract? Do you have any questions?"

"I read it several times and am happy with it. I have a flight in a couple of hours."

"Let's all sign," Helen says.

Everyone does, including documents authorizing Helen and Imogen to sign on behalf of the museum.

Helen faces Paris and extends her hand. Paris takes the hand in both his. It's not limp but not confident either. He wants to hug her. Actually, he wants to pollinate her. Perhaps she wants to be hugged and pollinated, but they settle on the handshake. His smile is turning into a laugh.

"To your success," Helen says.

"May delivery be as delicious as conception," Paris replies.

He's trying to suppress the laugh. He quickly gathers up papers and heads to the door. It's going to be a big fat neck-jerking laugh. He looks back at Helen. He can see that she notices him trying not to laugh.

She says, "Phone me to give me a time when you'll be arriving."

He leaves too fast while the others remain standing in the office. He has to get out of the room before the laugh explodes. He runs through reception and dashes out the glass door into the corridor. He can't keep it in any longer. He rounds the corner, leans back on the wall and lights up the hallway with what turns into a he-haw guffaw. His back sides down the wall until he's sitting on the floor. Two men in business suits waiting for the elevator look at him. Perhaps they'll call security.

"Penelope," he howls. "I'm coming home!"

Chapter Five

When Dr. Ernesto Adler receives a phone call from Helen advising him that the missing art might be returned, he can't contain his excitement.

"We don't want anyone to know," Helen says.

"Of course not!" he yells into the phone.

"They haven't been returned yet," Helen says, "but—"

"But you need me to get my money ready." His voice lowers. "Who is it? Who returned them?"

"We don't know." It isn't a lie, she tells herself, because she really doesn't know who Paris is, and she promised not to find out.

"Who met him? How did he make contact?"

"The police will handle it." If she had the slick mouth of a PR officer, she would be able to answer without answering while letting him believe she *had* answered.

His voice stammers as he tells her that he'll drop what he's doing in Palm Springs and take the next flight to Logan.

***

Lieutenant Lowell is in the bathroom for his morning ritual. You are what you eat, the saying goes, but Lowell knows it should be: you are what doesn't come out of you.

Lowell is a large man with an affable but not handsome face and thinning gray-brown hair. His nose, mouth, and ears are meant for a head even bigger than his. His pale skin accents his untrimmed eyebrows, protruding nose, and ear hair. To exercise his colon, his wife makes him porridge each morning to a consistency that keeps a jabbing spoon upright, and he adds 2 percent milk and three heaping spoons of brown sugar. He speaks with a broad Boston accent which interchanges the "A" and the "R."

He looks in the mirror and strokes his chin. He could say for certain that it isn't a bad-looking face, but it certainly isn't fresh.

He is wondering why on God's earth he should be selected to take over an art case? He understands the commissioner wanting someone new, but why him? Not that he knows too many cops who are art connoisseurs, but there must be someone who goes willingly to museums.

One person's taste in art should be as good as another's, which means that his taste counts the same as the museum director, except that he really can't say what his taste in art is. And why would anyone want to paint pictures these days when they could snap a photo and get an exact image? Isn't that what they aimed to do before they had cameras?

Lowell next wonders why there's movement on this case after all these years. Why didn't the robbers settle long ago and take the reward money? The statute of limitations ran out years ago, plus the police pledged that they would not prosecute on any grounds as long as the art is returned. But he also knows that criminals don't trust the police.

He should immediately get up to speed on the case and read about the investigations so far. Second, he should know something about the pictures that were robbed. It wouldn't hurt to know about art in general, Lowell thinks. The big plus on this case is not having to deal with police bureaucracy. In order to keep information from the news, he has to keep it from others in his department. He opens the bathroom door and jumps forward, ready for action.

By early morning, Lowell is in his office reading about the case. Many reports refer to the nefarious criminal Tizzio. Some experts don't believe that Tizzio has the art, but everyone agrees that he has something to do with the robbery. What can Lowell conclude from that? Criminal turf war? One thief double-crossing another?

By mid-afternoon he starts liking the idea of knowing about the pictures hanging on museum walls which thousands of people parade before in an almost religious reverence. He's seen it. He's been to the Louvre and watched people file past the *Mona Lisa*. They held their breath, cameras blazing, shocked by its size.

He remembers seeing a real Rembrandt in another museum in Germany, or was it Holland? It hung in between a bunch of crucifixion pictures. Yes, he would learn all about art in the next couple of days.

He'll dig into the archives and search online. After the paintings are returned, the commissioner wants him to find the thief, who may be the ever-elusive Tizzio.

***

After Paris's plane lands in Albuquerque, he dashes straight off to Apollo Self Storage across the Rio Grande, runs upstairs and pays homage to his statues of Athena, Apollo, and Orpheus. He thanks Athena and rethanks her until his knees buckle and he's in tears. What a blessing. "Oh Athena, daughter of Zeus and Metis, granddaughter of Gaia, you have restored me. I will not fail you this time!"

There's a lot to be done, and he sets to work, putting a box on his desk and packing his books. Most of his furniture and belongings he will either throw away or drop off at Goodwill, but he cannot live without his books and papers.

Boxes and packing tape are right there in his office, so all he has to do is fill and tape the boxes. When he's finished packing, he'll go to storage unit B-33 and take care of the crate containing hundreds of millions of dollars of art and his passport to a new life.

Midway in his packing, he phones Alice. They never quite split up after she divorced him. She filed the papers; he signed them. For the past months, whenever either would see an interesting article or a funny internet picture, they forwarded the page to the other, both knowing the relationship would never again get beyond forwarding articles.

"It's going good," he answers to her greetings. "Actually, it's going real good. I feel like I haven't felt since I started at Princeton."

He strolls around with the phone on his ear.

"I'm going to present Pythagoras to the world. He wanted beauty in the world. Look at the crassness of society.

He wanted—"

"Stop."

"Right. I'm too excited. I may have a chance to make up for the pain I caused, the mistakes I made."

"Will it be different for you or will you repeat the same pattern in a different field?"

"I swore an oath to Athena not to be cocky or selfish. I've got it all worked out. It isn't a petty thing. I can't tell you more about it yet."

Paris is happily gesturing as he talks. "I've got Clarise working here full time. In fact, Barry is selling the storage business for me. I'm moving to Boston."

Alice is silent.

Paris says, "I just want to apologize. My thing of fooling the world was like being an alcoholic—once I had a taste of being superior to others, I couldn't stop. But now the gods are smiling on me again. Patience in adversity. I remember a dream—maybe it wasn't a dream but a wish—that the goddess Eos came to me at dawn and presented me an empty platter, like a new start. The gods have responded in abundance."

"I wish you luck," Alice says. "From the bottom of my heart."

Paris feels her sincerity.

She adds, "It took a long time to get over you. I don't know if it's that we were mismatched or that just you are mismatched."

"Thanks, Alice. You're an exceptional person. Nothing wrong with being mismatched."

After he hangs up, he goes to a drawer where he has designs he made of temples and ancient sites. He once drew what the Pythagorean colony in Croton, Southern Italy, must have looked like. He thought about throwing them away—as he had thrown away so many other projects while he was on trial. Now they will be used.

He also sees a black-and-white eight-by-ten photo of James Bond in a tux, the only image of modernity he owns, and he puts it with his drawings. He's read every Ian Fleming novel and seen every Bond film. The Bond myth is the modern Odysseus legend. The hero is cool, clever, brave, effective. The exaggerated stories recounted by Homer are the same as the exaggerated stories of Bond. When he's alone and not using Odysseus's imaginary bow, he talks to beautiful Bond-esque women. His fooling the scholarly world was very James Bond, truth be known.

His friend Barry knocks, enters and looks around. He has the air of a competent clerk whose hands are used to being wrapped around a bottle of beer. Except for trimming his brown beard, he pays as little attention to his appearance as Paris does.

Barry notices on the desk printouts about stock, option, and futures investing. "When you first told me, I thought it was another of your crazy dreams."

"I thought the same."

"I'm going to miss bullshitting with you, but I'm glad you're going rather than withering away here. I don't need to tell you that if you need anything..."

"I'll invite you to Boston as soon as I can. Know my dream of a temple on top of a hill? It might not be far off. A beacon that will help take us to a world of multi-possibilities. We drifted away from science. Electrons and plastics are determining our world. Science should never be subservient to technology. We need to return to our base."

"Like I said, I'm going to miss your bullshit."

"Alice thinks I'm too obstinate to change, but I'll be putting into practice the books I read, the thoughts I had."

"Be good to yourself this time."

"It won't be for me. It will be a gift *from* me. There's a lot of interest in Pythagoras. My book was a best seller. People want to know for the sake of knowing."

His sermon is interrupted by the sound of a car driving up and squealing to a stop. Two guys rush into the office.

"There's a Jolly Green Giant for you," one of them announces as Paris opens the door.

The other says, "He's from Texas. Says he can pin you to the ground in half a minute flat. Says he's never lost."

"I've got work to do," Paris says. "I don't have time to wrestle some narcissist."

His protests are feeble. They boisterously pull him and Barry past the door and into their car. They speed to a neighborhood pub that serves as an after-work hangout for the spread-out community on the other side of the Rio Grande from Albuquerque. Rock music comes from an old-fashioned jukebox. Thirty-year-olds are in groups drinking and joking.

Everyone stops when the guys enter. One woman bounds up to Paris and takes off his jacket, pulling him forward toward the large empty middle of the room. Two others move chairs to create an empty circle while another two people unfold a padded, gray wrestling mat in the center of the circle. Everyone gathers around as the chatter builds. The woman behind the bar pours drinks at a hectic pace, rushing from one end of the bar to the other.

Barry, notepad in hand, jumps in and begins taking bets as people hand him money left and right. The din rises. Paris enjoys the attention. The Texan wrestler—wearing a top that emphasizes his tattooed muscles—stands near the bar, and when someone points to Paris, the wrestler is beside himself with laughter.

"I'm supposed to be scared of him?" He walks up to Paris, stands two feet away, and inspects him closely.

"Everyone says the same thing," Barry says. "But look who they have their money on."

The wrestler remains incredulous.

"They're betting on how long it takes," Barry says.

The wrestler says to Barry, "I whipped everyone's ass in the slammer."

"So did he."

"No shit?"

"I was there," Barry says. He points to one of the guys. "He's the referee."

The two men prepare to wrestle on the mat, taking off

their belts, shoes, and shirts. They stand opposite each other, a Harley rider from Texas versus an athletic-built ranting intellectual.

When Paris and the wrestler walk onto the mat, their difference in size is clear. People are whistling and hollering.

The referee approaches and puts a hand on each shoulder. "You both know the rules. Clean. Begin."

The people squeeze around the scene yelling encouragement. Most have beers in their hands: others have bills though their knuckles. The two contenders walk in a circle around the mat eyeing each other. Paris is relaxed and observant. The wrestler makes aggressive lunges toward Paris but holds back. The crowd around them are clapping and yelling, making noise for the two to make contact.

The bartender shouts to Paris, "Knock him off balance."

The wrestler puts his arms around Paris's shoulders, but before he has a chance to lock in position, Paris ducks under the wrestler's big arms and crawls out. They keep waiting for the other to make the first move. The crowd becomes louder.

"Grab his leg!" another person shouts to Paris. "Quick."

"Let him come after you," another says.

The wrestler and Paris lock arms and continue turning faster and faster, the referee turning with them. The wrestler uses his power to throw Paris on his side, but as he shifts his weight, Paris ducks, grabs the back of his opponent's knee and bends it forward. The wrestler falls straight to the mat, and in one fluid motion, Paris grabs the wrestler's arm and twists it to lock. He brings down his knee on the Texan's other shoulder, pinning it to the mat.

The referee drops to his knee and confirms. The crowd howls. Paris lets the stunned wrestler go. Barry comes over and offers his hands to bring the Texan to his feet. Paris shakes the dismayed man's hand.

"I've never seen that type of wrestling," he says about

Paris' swift polished gesture.

"Been around for three thousand years."

"You'd be rich if you did this for a living."

"Money ruined athletics." Paris is smug. "It ruins everything. In ancient times 25 percent of the people were enslaved. Now it's more like 95 percent are slaves to money."

The wrestler reaches into his pocket and hands Barry a couple of hundred-dollar bills. Barry turns around: "Pitchers all around."

The people in the bar yell approval and thanks. A couple of them come up and pat Paris on the back. One returns Paris's shirt and belt as he stands at the bar.

The wrestler points at Paris and asks Barry, "Friend of yours?"

"We met inside."

"How did you get time?"

"Computer stuff."

"And him?"

"Broke into a professor's office. Didn't like his research methodology."

***

When Paris and Barry return to Apollo Self Storage, they stuff clothes in Barry's car so he can drop them at the Goodwill collection kiosk.

The two shake hands and give each other a light hug, as much as men do in that situation. Paris takes the Apollo statue off its pedestal and hands it to Barry who leaves with robust good wishes.

Paris wants to finish packing, load the crate of art, and start driving before Clarise, his part-time employee, comes to work. He overstuffs his garbage bin with things no one would want—the majority of his possessions. He loads his boxes in the van, making sure to leave a space in the back for the crate of art. Attorney Rothman warned him to handle the goods as little as possible since they may have evidence. He walks downstairs in the dark to unit B-33 with a flashlight.

Panic. Both locks have been changed. He's sure of it.

He drops everything in his hands, rushes up to unit 33 and grabs each lock. For sure they've been changed. He rushes back into his apartment for small tools to pick the locks, realizes they're packed away and then tries to remember in which box. Five hundred million dollars worth of art, and he didn't take the slightest precaution when he left for Boston. He runs back to the van and, like a madman, throws things out until he finds the box of tools, which he had put on the bottom since it's heavy. He rips open the box and turns it upside down, scattering his tools on the ground and then pulling out a tumble pick. He runs back to unit 33, stumbling over his keys on the ground. He points his flashlight and bends down to gather them up, and then rushes in and turns on the motion detector lights. What if the keys work in the locks? His hands are so shaky that he drops the keys again, picks them up and tries them in the locks.

They work. He had forgotten he'd put on new locks. He opens the overhead door and sees the crate inside. Everything looks normal. Nerves. Fear of success—a healthy attitude for those who follow ancient customs. Success can attract the evil eye.

***

Paris straightens his mess, loads the crate into the van, and begins his U-Haul drive on Interstate 40. He's nibbling on olives and cheese from a deli counter and listening to Bellini's opera *Norma*. He stops for the night near Memphis, backs up to a motel room and eats a traditional Tennessee dinner from an all-night restaurant across the street, his eye on his van. He starts up again at first light next morning.

That evening, after he sees a sign welcoming him to Abingdon, Virginia, he flicks his turn signal and pulls off the expressway, turning toward a motel next to a filling station. A buzzer goes off as Paris opens the office door. He sees born-again Christian posters on the wall. A disheveled geezer emerges from the back room and stands behind the counter. Paris asks for a room while hearing a game show from the television in the back room.

The motel keeper reaches for a key behind him and then puts it on the counter. "Number seven. Costs forty-nine ninety-five, plus one-forty for the governor."

Paris pays cash.

"Where you headed?"

"Boston."

"I mean, where you really headed? I can tell you ain't a believer. Otherwise, you'd share your faith with a fellow Christian."

"Christian? The hoard that trampled a great civilization and replaced it with doggerel and stick-figure art?"

The motel keeper looks baffled. "Maybe you one of those intellectuals: all thought and no guts. They got plenty of them in Boston, but we're righteous God-fearing folks here."

"In a forgotten world people once tried to discover. Then they stopped trying because they knew, and it took other courageous people to admit ignorance and return to discovery. Now we have people who know, like you, and the ignorant, like me."

Paris picks up the key, issues a plastic smile, turns and walks out while feeling the motel keeper's hard eye on him.

There are two cars in the courtyard. Paris backs up in front of unit seven, stops the engine, gets out and unlocks his motel room door. He can see the motel keeper looking out the window at him. At least the room is clean, and he can get a decent night's sleep. He shouldn't have engaged that crazy fellow. Stay focused. Deliver the paintings.

He thinks about Edward Gibbon, his most admirable classical scholar, who wrote expressive prose and filled his history with astonishing—often cuttingly witty—opinions. In his cocky days, Paris dreamed of updating Gibbon's work in Gibbon's style. A lot more is known now about the classical period than Gibbon knew in the early eighteenth century, thanks to scholars, archeologists, and serendipitous finds, including Paris's real discoveries.

Next morning, Paris, day bag in hand, opens his door and yawns, looking out and above at the coming day. By the end of the day, he will deliver his load and begin a new life. All of a sudden he notices a "Righteousness Rocks" bumper sticker on the back of the U-Haul. He drops his bag in panic and rushes to open the truck, searching his pockets for the key, realizing that he has left the key inside. He runs into the room and grabs the key. His heart is racing. A half billion dollars was sitting in the back of the truck. One crazy monotheist. Art means nothing to them; they burned art and books and then burned the artists and authors. His hand is jumpy as he puts the key into the lock on the truck's back door. No telling what a zealous monotheist would do.

He sees the crate in order, his baggage surrounding it, just as he had loaded it, and breathes a sigh of relief. Second panic in two days. Freudian counter-intention. He looks at the motel office and believes he sees a curtain slide open enough for the motel keeper to peer out the window at him. He says to himself disparagingly, "Monotheists: they ruin everything." It's an opinion he shares with Gibbon.

The gods are warning him to keep his caustic feelings to himself. He has to stop being his own worst enemy and make sure he doesn't blow this divine gift.

***

Haggard-looking, eyes glazed from the long drive, Paris enters Massachusetts well after dark and phones Helen to give an estimated time of arrival.

"I'll tell everyone to meet at the warehouse," Helen says.

"I'm looking forward to seeing you again." A feeble statement, but he was too road weary to come up with anything cool.

"We'll get to meet Lieutenant Lowell."

Two hours later Paris arrives at the loading platform of the warehouse in Jamaica Plain, backing the U-Haul to the platform.

Director Imogen, Lieutenant Lowell, and attorney Rothman are waiting with Helen. Paris steps out and looks around to make sure there's no one else. Is he being unduly paranoid? He knows that Helen is capable of organizing secrecy.

Helen introduces Lowell. The two men stand opposite each other sizing up the other. Lowell has a happy face. Paris, although tired, is also happy that all is going according to plan.

"I'll give you the rest of the evening to unwind, then we can meet tomorrow morning," Lowell says.

"I want to help nail the thief and get the money back to Helen."

The women help Paris carry the crate through the loading door and into the warehouse office. Rothman and Lowell guide them, Lowell making comments about the muscles of his latissimus dorsi and the possibility of upsetting an inguinal hernia.

They put the crate in the center of the empty room. Paris pulls out a Wonderbar from his back pocket. Helen stands in a dignified mixture of excitement and nervousness. Imogen takes a step back and hands Helen a pair of examination gloves. When he pries open the crate, both women dive toward it. Their hands become cautious as soon as they're inside the crate, carefully putting their fingers on a canvas and pulling out *The Sea of Galilee*. It is a Rembrandt of a calm Jesus surrounded by alarmed disciples in a boat tossed by a wave. The light, the flow, the faces, the emotion it transmits is tremendous. Rembrandt, a true artist who spurned those who didn't appreciate his art, including his benefactors, created a school of artists, making it hard to know which paintings were his or his students.

They examine it. "That's it. That's it."

Imogen, crowding next to Helen's shoulder, confirms. They both study the picture, its paint strokes, its cut edge. They turn it over and look at the back. The hardest job of a forger is to reproduce the back since they need to have the painting in hand and see what's on the reverse. Museums never show that.

Rothman says, "It's better to keep your opinions until they've been authenticated."

"I know this is it," Helen says. "When you feel the art, you know it's real."

"So true," Paris says.

"You process the image in your brain but feel it in your gut," Lowell says. "Reality is a mind-body experience."

"I was struck by it when I first touched it," Paris says.

Helen and Imogen take out Vermeer's *The Concert*. It is a painting of two women playing instruments on either side of a brawny-shouldered man who shows only his back. Vermeer's sense of light dominates the scene. No one used light as he did.

"This is it too!" Helen yells out.

"No doubt," Imogen says.

Rothman says, "If I'm not mistaken, what you have in your hand is worth over two hundred million."

"Everyone wants to put a price on art," Helen says. "Art and money should have nothing in common."

"Except to the robbers," Lowell replies. "And now to us."

Paris says, "Money and art always intertwine. Even in the classical age artists vied for state support. They had contests—the prize was money."

Rothman brings out documents and a camera. Paris moves away. Helen and Imogen hold up each canvas while Rothman snaps pictures.

People sign Rothman's documents without looking at them. Rothman says, "Let's meet in my office on Thursday at noon for disbursement or refutation of authenticity."

Everyone agrees. Helen walks to Paris, standing close. "How can we thank you?"

"Ten million dollars is a damn good start."

Chapter Six

When Helen walks into her office the next morning, she finds Dr. Adler standing near the bookshelf thumbing through one of her art books. She keeps a working office—her design—a modern glass desk that visitors face when they enter and a library of art reference books on the left, books that look often used. Every object is tactfully placed, even the canvases and frames on the floor.

Not only does she lecture on aesthetics, she lives it. The sign on her office door reads, *Flowers Before Bread.* Her purpose is art, and her objective is elevating human creativity.

No one is better in her job than she. No one is more respected by rich and poor, liberal and conservative. She seems to know everybody everywhere, calls them by name, has an inviting handshake, a polite, sensitive smile.

Dr. Adler is dressed in a formally casual sports jacket befitting a museum trustee and dealer in fine art, the silk scarf of a sophisticated middle-aged gentleman tucked under his loose collar.

"I'm so sorry to keep you waiting," she says.

"On the contrary, I should have phoned your assistant when my plane landed but I couldn't help rushing here as soon as you told me this wonderful news."

"You're so terrific—your generosity and quick action. Only because of you did other donors come forward and post the initial reward."

"If your news is true, it will be the best ten million we ever spent. I'll have my half of the money ready tomorrow. Do we need cash?"

"A check will do."

"Then the person returning the art doesn't mind being traced?"

"The attorney will be handling it. You won't find a

more tight-lipped persona than Rothman."

"I know."

He walks around, turns to her and says, "I love the museum."

Helen has heard Dr. Adler voice his love for the museum many times, and each time she hears a greater enthusiasm than from any other trustee.

He looks right at her and lowers his voice. "Who is it? Do we have the scoundrels?"

"We may be close."

"Wonderful. The paintings—you're sure they're authentic?"

"Absolutely."

"How did we get them?"

Be diplomatic, she tells herself. Don't give away Paris's identity even to the wonderful Dr. Adler.

"It's now in police hands."

"Perhaps one of the gang gave up and wanted the reward?"

"We're not sure." She assures herself that it's an utterly true statement.

"I'm terribly excited. I cried continuously for three weeks after the theft. What can we do to help the police?"

"I'd stay out of their way; they suspect everyone who approaches them, even to help."

"How can anyone possibly suspect me?" Slight chuckle.

"I know it's absurd."

"We must go out of our way to help the police grab those scoundrels. I heard there's a new police investigator. I can offer the contacts I've made in the art underworld. What's his name?"

She wonders why Paris was so adamant about keeping information from Dr. Adler. Does Paris have a reason to fear Dr. Adler? She also wonders how Dr. Adler knew so quickly about the new investigator. Rothman admonished them not to divulge information.

She knows that Dr. Adler is hopeless at details, seeking the broad canvas over individual brush strokes. Like Helen, this gallant man can never be an artist himself because he cannot sit still and work each section of a painting, each chisel of the marble. He seeks the worldview and leaves the dusting and accounting to others.

Dr. Adler loves her sense of style, her way with prudent words, her diplomacy. He suggested that she write a Ms. Manners column. He calls her his Angel of Delphi, in contrast to the often ill-pronouncing Oracle.

"The police commissioner is keeping everything on a need-to-know basis for now, but we'll probably have the chance to meet the investigator. Then you can help him with your extensive contacts."

"And all of the items have been returned?"

Helen nods. "That's the most important thing, isn't it? That we have everything back. Oh but one thing is missing: the Samos vase."

"Ah. Maybe that's because it didn't fit with the rest of the art?"

"Probably."

"It's not important. I'm so happy, but I won't rest until those scalawags are punished. I'd like to lash them to a pillory in the middle of Copley Square and allow the citizens of Boston to whip them for all the misery they brought the city."

"Let's keep positive, Dr. Adler; the art has been recovered!"

Adler bows, shakes her hand gallantly and leaves.

***

Lieutenant Lowell, dressed in a frumpy sports jacket over an open-collar shirt, is sitting at a table in front of a window in Helen's apartment overlooking Washington Park.

The apartment is as strategically decorated as the museum, with dried flowers, art books, and the *New Yorker* placed on polished tables. Colors match. Lines and curves flow into each other. Light is used precisely to enhance the expression of beauty. Helen has the knack of blending opposite art styles, a heavy Italian Renaissance canvas behind an Art Deco chair, an Impressionist watercolor next to a colonial era highboy. Like Isabella, Helen's unconventional taste works brilliantly.

Lowell is between two empty chairs; Helen is preparing light snacks in the kitchen. Paris enters, and Lowell stands. Both men are smiling—Lowell large and slightly rotund, Paris loose and cheery. Helen introduces the men again while they shake hands. Paris sees Lowell studying him as they sit, but his geniality makes Paris feel comfortable.

He tells Lowell that he just unloaded his books and few belongings in a Somerville storage unit similar to the one he owns.

"We're awaiting official word from our staff about the art's authenticity," Helen says, "which should come this afternoon. Our restorers know the paintings intimately, the exact stitches per inch of the canvas, each pin prick on the back, the X-rayed sketches underneath them."

When asked, both Lowell and Paris tell her they prefer tea. She goes off to brew it.

"Helen tells me that you're a classical scholar," Lowell begins. "Can you tell me what you do with that?"

"Do you ask astronomers what they do with the knowledge that there are different types of galaxies in the universe? There's isn't much you can do with basic knowledge. But we all want to know who we are, how we got here. I study where our civilization came from. It's like studying evolution but focusing on the last twenty-five hundred years rather than the eight million years since we were related to chimpanzees."

"Good point."

"The art in our museum is also a tribute to history," Helen says from the kitchen.

"A lot of people believe that history isn't relevant," Paris says. "University history departments exist marginally. Industrial societies worship business and technology. Classical studies is laughed at by academics. What can it add to our lives? But history is not about those who lived in the past. It's about us. We read history to find out about our own motivations and lusts."

Neither Lowell nor Helen interrupts him, so he continues broadcasting.

"We want to understand how humans behave. Caesar is not different from leaders today. Men went to war for the same reasons they go to war today. People fell in love for the same reasons as they do today, and there was just as much unrequited love and jealousy and sexual turmoil. We race to find life on distant planets and in the depths of the oceans hoping to understand more about ourselves. We need to know who we are and what we're doing here."

He's sitting on the edge of his seat opposite Lowell.

"I'm a historian of the classical world because I want to know why we want to know. I'm pretty sure that dogs and zebras are not possessed with this desire to know what we're doing here. Other animals concentrate on survival."

"Anxiety is the leading cause of irritable bowl syndrome," Lowell says.

Paris's puzzlement stops his own rant. Helen reenters the room with a tray.

Lowell says, "Let's start at the beginning. The Gardner Museum heist of 1990. You have any first or second-hand knowledge of that?"

"Of course not. I would never steal from Helen."

"Thank you," Helen says. She puts tea in front of each person and sits.

"This thug named Jason comes up to the desk. What a dunce. He didn't even know about Jason and the Argonauts, the first Jason being sent by King Aeëtes to search for the fleece."

Lowell shakes his head. "You lost me. Who got fleeced?"

"Hercules refused to head the expedition, so it fell to Jason. Few people know the story."

"Jason?"

"Unlike the ancient Jason, this guy was a big thug: thug

hands, thug brain. He's so dense light bends around him."

"Why did you suspect him?"

"The way he scanned the room. I fished through his storage unit."

"It was locked, I assume."

He nods. "Later Hercules killed his music teacher."

"And you found the paintings?"

"I read how Isabella Stewart Gardner labored with her own sweat to establish a place for the spiritual well-being of others. Then some thug like Jason comes along. It's like robbing Santa Claus."

"Do you need protection?"

"Only if it comes out that I broke into his unit. Jason is one of those small-eyed men with fat stomachs who pushes himself to the front of a line, who doesn't care if everyone thinks he's nasty—who thrives on people thinking he's nasty—and everyone lets him have his way rather than wasting energy on confrontation, which just makes him more belligerent ."

He looks over at Helen and a warm feeling surges inside him. She's kind, soft, sophisticated. A self-contained lady. Not fragile or dependent. He wants to be near her, not just today. But she comes from class, and he is no good at pretending to belong to her class.

He says to Lowell, "They can't trace me because the storage business isn't in my name."

"Whose name is the business in?"

"I had to buy the business under a friend's name."

"Why is that?"

"Because...well...because of several reasons. It's kind of like a trust."

Should he say that it's in the name of his ex-probation officer? Not in front of Helen. Lowell would find out right away. He sizes up Lowell. He's a guy who listens, observes. He may sound off-the-wall, his broad Boston accent, his physicality, but he knows how to get to the bottom of things. He is a master of his destiny, a captain of his soul.

"Does anyone else know?"

"One person I trust, a computer wiz, hacker, but he doesn't do that anymore. I changed the locks on Jason's unit so no one can get in. The guy comes about every six months, opens the place wearing gloves and looks in."

"Jason will be looking for you if we don't find him first."

"I used to be in academia. I'm traceable there, but I doubt that he would read a philosophical treatise on Peloponnesus goddess worship. I thought I should leave New Mexico. I've been thinking about Boston."

He glances at Helen to see how she takes this news but he doesn't see a reaction. Perhaps he shouldn't see her again until he's cut his past and made something of his gift from her.

He gives Lowell the information that Barry gave him about Jason and the rental car. Paris notices that Lowell does not take notes.

"If we don't tell anyone that the paintings have been returned, the thief won't know either."

"You reckon he's rich?"

"I have that feeling."

"Did that feeling happen in your throat, in your chest, or in your belly?"

"What?"

"We think that feelings just come out of nowhere, but feelings come from the body, and different parts of the body produce different feelings."

"How am I supposed to know what body part? It's animal nature."

"You get sensitive to how the body works. Specific chemicals are released for different emotions. They go to different parts of the body then excite the brain. We are the body."

Paris thinks, well here you have it, a ranter about history facing a man fixated on the body. And Helen does her best to take it all in.

When Paris and Lowell are halfway out the door, Helen says to Paris, "Tomorrow is your big day."

Betraying his rational nature, Paris says, "The goddess Luna will be bright tomorrow night, a gift of Diana. Can I see you again?"

She nods. He winks and watches her shut the door after them.

***

At nine the next morning, Paris, Helen, Imogen, and Lieutenant Lowell are ushered into attorney Rothman's office in downtown Boston. Helen and Paris look at each other, silently laugh, look away. Paris nervously rolls and unrolls his legal contract. He notices that Helen's eyes are wide and bright—even Imogen is brimming with a rare open smile.

Rothman greets everyone with a handshake across his desk. Paris sits on one end and Helen on the other, with Lowell and Imogen in the middle of the semicircle of chairs. They begin chatting about incidentals—the change in climate, Boston's role in the Revolutionary War, the Old North Church, which British soldiers tore apart to keep their campfires warm against the New England winter.

Lowell gives a brief lecture on the difference between glucose, dextrose, galactose, multose, lactose, sucrose, and fructose, the last being the most sweet and most addictive.

Finally Rothman announces that the returned art has been authenticated, which everyone already knew, but his declaration gives a potent finality.

"You're now a rich man, Mr. Paris," Rothman says. "Be forewarned, people who suddenly acquire wealth usually don't do well, either with their money or their personal lives."

"I have already made investment plans. One request is for you to hold up some of the money and make a cash purchase for real estate in Boston in the name of the nonprofit I'm starting."

He hands Rothman papers regarding his nonprofit and investments.

"So you'll be moving here?" Imogen asks.

The annoyance in her tone doesn't derail the festive atmosphere.

"I've already started looking."

Rothman looks over Paris's papers. One sheet drops from his hand. Paris starts to bend down to pick it up for him. Lowell stops him with an outstretched hand. "When we get excited, the intestinal microflora becomes overactive. Reversing the normal pull of gravity causes the intestinal juices to whirl around where they shouldn't."

He himself bends down and picks up the paper and hands it back to Rothman.

Helen brings out a bottle of French champagne. Rothman asks his secretary to bring in six glasses. They stand and engage in more nervous chatter. Paris is so happy he doesn't know what to say except to quote odd and irrelevant lines of Greek drama. Ten. Million. Dollars. Helen is standing in front of him, and she is all he wants to look at.

Rothman pops the cork and pours.

Paris proposes a toast. "By the light of Apollo—to art."

The others toast the museum, Rembrandt, Vermeer, the police department, the ladies' talkative cab driver—whose wife just had a baby—and the small intestine.

"You have the art." Paris raises his right arm. "By Hercules, I swear an oath that you'll have the thief."

Lowell and Paris turn toward each other and raise their glasses in a private toast. "To the capture of the thief."

Chapter Seven

As soon as Lieutenant Lowell lands in New Mexico, he becomes concerned about the dry air sapping the moisture out of his nasal cavity. He tilts his head back, squirts Afrin into his nose and holds it closed. It is after dark. He wonders what his sinuses are going to feel like in sunshine.

The local police greet him planeside and take him directly to Apollo Self Storage. Lowell immediately recognizes the cop staking out the place; even a middle-of-the-road thief would take one look and continue driving. He thinks that when they heard from the Boston commissioner, they overreacted to make sure they made no mistakes. Lowell observes that the building on a frontage road off the main highway is mildly well trafficked; no one could observe all the cars that drive by.

The local police lead him by flashlight and show him how they examined the now-empty storage unit where the paintings were discovered. He sees that they did a professional job.

"We did it at night so no one saw us," one of the cops says.

"The girl who works here?"

"Doesn't know anything. We'll keep an eye out for her. What's this about? Homicide?"

Lowell says that he can't disclose.

"Drugs? They all use units like this."

Lowell examines the record book kept on the office desk. It dates back two years—to the time Paris bought the business.

"I'd like to talk to the previous owner," Lowell says.

"He died. It was a business for a retired guy to pass the time. That's why the current owner bought it cheap: the family wanted to unload it. The old guy didn't believe in records, except for one pretty useless log. He didn't know how to use a computer. It seems he did most things by memory, probably to dodge the IRS. He made it seem like the business didn't make money. He never wrote down ID numbers, just took the money. Kept most in cash."

The cop hands Lowell all the papers.

"So we don't know when this renter started using unit B-33?"

"Perhaps he checked out other storage places until he found one that was an easy touch."

Another cop says, "We should have a lab report this week. Crime swabbed the place last night using construction lights."

Lowell thinks about what Paris said, that the guy wore gloves and didn't enter the place, just stood outside looking at the crate all covered up. It was a long shot to start with that they'd be able to find any evidence from the space, but it's procedure. He's already had his people in Boston work over the crate, the locks, the nails, and the tarp. The locks came through a Home Depot supplier in the Southwest. The wood is from Canada and sold at every Home Depot in the country. There's nothing on the tarp yet, except that the lab reckons that it's about five years old.

Lowell likes to get the feel of things by actually being there. He thinks about his odor-detection idea, sensitive enough to detect the molecules which emit from the mouth—from which most molecules are emitted—and have an exact imprint of the person's internal organs. The guy breathed into this closed space. The first thing you'd have to do for the odor-detection principal would be to take an air sample before everyone else's organs extract their signature.

"Must be big if they're sending you down here to investigate," one of the cops says to Lowell, his voice betraying his hope for more information.

The other cop says, "We get cases of people who don't pay their storage rent. After nine months the owner files a report and gets the right to break into the unit and sell whatever is inside."

Lowell gets a feeling in his gut that there won't be any more information at the site, meaning that he'll have to wait six months until the renter returns.

***

A real estate agent unlocks the front door and begins showing Paris the hollow space on the seventh and eighth floor of a factory building. The agent looks bored, like he's wasting his time; Paris doesn't look like the type who can afford such a place. The large open space, two stories high and half the size of a football field, used to be a factory with solid brick walls and high I-beam ceilings. Although it isn't a tall building, it has a vast view of the city through wall-to-wall windows. The floor, walls, and ceiling are rough, as if the owners had gruffly pulled out all their equipment and disappeared. Boxes of nails, sacks of cement mix, and a bucket of joint compound are lying around. The rest is an unsightly empty shell. The outside needs to be sandblasted and restored. Paris has the listing sheet in his hand.

"Panoramic view." The agent's voice is unenthusiastic.

Yes. Paris thinks of Panorama, the Macedonian town on a hill north of Thessalonica. Alexander the Great must have walked up there in his youth and looked out at the sea thinking of his coming conquests. Panorama's extraordinary view over Thessalonica and the Mediterranean is just like the space Paris is looking at, a view of Boston on one side and the harbor on the other side.

Paris looks around, pointing to a corner. "This can be the symposia. Yes, that'll be quite fine when it's finished."

"It's up to the buyer to finish it the way he likes. That's what you told me you wanted. Have you been pre-qualified or pre-approved?"

Paris is thinking that he can run a twenty-foot-wide second floor around the perimeter and keep the center open for the full two floors, creating a spacious octahedron central area, one of the shapes Pythagoras enjoyed. He already has a design for it.

He notices the agent staring at him. "Pre what?"

"For the mortgage. You also need a substantially larger down payment and deposit since the place is bare and raw. The bank will want to see that funds are available to finish the place."

"Oh yes, that's all fine." He continues looking, imagining.

"And with what bank?"

Paris jumps up and down to test the floor. "Rock solid," he says.

"You can put the Queen Elisabeth on it. They had large machines here, so the place has extra structural supports. What's the bank?"

Paris, pointedly not responding to the agent's sarcasm, sizes up the large open space with its grand view. "Marble flooring throughout." He looks at another corner. "That can be an area for scribes." He says to the agent, "The library. Pythagoras and Socrates argued against reading and writing because it reduced memory, but we have to incorporate modern ideas."

"Whatever. This place is like a blank slate. What's the name of the bank?"

Paris walks around, examines the walls trying to imagine how he can turn it into a Pythagorean museum. The agent looks increasingly annoyed.

"A statue of Apollo there. The Pythagorean school at Croton was dedicated to Apollo. We can put a fresco of Aphrodite and Hera over here. A few columns leading to this splendid view. I can open that part up, take out the wall and replace it with a row of ceiling-supporting statues. This can be the musical theory area. We can install a skylight in the center for astronomical viewing. The Pythagoreans observed the heavens; they calculated that the planets moved around the sun."

That's something he can't blame on the monotheists: it was other Greeks who established an Earth-centered universe.

Paris keeps looking around. "This is definitely the best

possibility I've seen—a modern temple on a hill."

The agent doesn't get it. He looks at his watch while Paris looks at the listing sheet. "Taxes, ah-ha, maintenance fee, ah-ha. But I don't see the price."

"It hasn't changed since I told you at the office; two point four nine."

"Steep, but a good place."

"I'm glad you like it."

"I'll take it."

"The down payment, the mortgage?"

"That won't be necessary. Cash. Two point one. Not one cent more. Close in two weeks." He walks around. "I'll come by your office, sign the papers and give you a deposit in an hour. I'd first like to stay and think about putting in a fountain. A Temple of the Muses must have a fountain."

Paris's wry smile. The agent's shocked face.

The agent suddenly becomes polite. "Sir, I'll be waiting for you."

He turns to leave. Paris taps him on the shoulder and stands right in front of his face. "When you judge a statue, look through the marble and feel its *psyche*. The same for a person."

***

Worrying about the low car seat cramping his intestine and numbing his kidneys, Lowell takes a painfully long five-hour drive to the car rental agency in Flagstaff. He phones his boss from the car and tells him that it's a serious situation when the digestive juices remain stifled. "The intestinal microvilli are subjected to inactivity, curbing the enzymes' ability to pass nutrients into the blood."

A woman smoking a cigarette outside the rental office tells him to come in; she'll be right inside. Lowell shakes his arms and legs to circulate the blood while waiting until she finishes her nicotine-fueled break. She enters, blowing a large smoky breath into the room. He ducks.

Lowell has medical books from the 1930s that claim that smoking after a meal promotes good digestion. This is why he insists on reading double-blind medical studies.

He shows his badge and gives her the car's license plate number and date he's looking for.

She brings it up on the computer.

"Name: Donald Jason. Arizona driver's license. He paid cash."

Naturally, Lowell thinks.

"Did he hold the reservation with a credit card?"

"Yeah, but the card info gets automatically wiped out if we don't use it." She gives him the driver's license number, street address, and phone number—information Lowell already had, courtesy of Paris's hacker friend Barry.

"And I guess the car's been cleaned, inside and out?"

"Every time. It's been rented three times since. We don't have many cars, so when someone rents a standard or midsize and we don't have it, we give them a luxury one like the MKS."

He thanks her and then drives to police headquarters on Stone Street. He's directed to a jovial detective who is eager to help because he got his criminology degree from Bridgewater State University south of Boston. A few minutes with the detective on his computer proves Barry correct. He shows Lowell a picture of the real Donald Jason from the Arizona Department of Transportation website.

All Lowell has is Paris's physical description of the thug masquerading as Donald Jason, which describes half of all robust white males in their late thirties.

When Lowell returns to New Mexico, another belly-cruncher of a trip, he meets Paris's parole officer who tells him the story of Paris's incarceration. Paris couldn't get a loan to buy the storage business, so the parole officer, taken by Paris's humility, put it in his own name in a private agreement with Paris. It was one of the parole officer's few success stories. He gives Lowell the address of Alice, Paris's ex-wife.

Lowell rings her doorbell and asks about her relationship with Paris without telling her why he wants to know.

She invites him into the sitting room. Lowell avoids

the divan which reminds him too much of a car seat. He takes an upright armchair, sticking his fingers under his right ribcage to massage his liver.

"We traveled," she tells him, "We never went to Disneyland or the Cote d'Azure. Nothing about being with him was easy. Like Odysseus, adventure runs in his blood. He didn't make hotel reservations. We might've been camping or biking or hiking to some long-forgotten ruin, and there won't be anything relaxed about the experience. He became known in academia as the 'slogging scholar'."

Lowell hears nostalgia in her voice.

"We took public transportation or walked, even if we didn't know where we were going. Then we'd set off to some ancient site that'd been abandoned for twenty-five hundred years. We'd carry our luggage, sleep in the open, walk where there wasn't a trail. If it rained, we wouldn't have umbrellas. We'd get lost, never take a car because the ancients didn't have them. We'd cook lentils and rice over a fire, drink water from a creek."

"Why did you stay with him?"

"I just told you why."

"You mean you enjoyed getting wet, sleeping with mosquitoes, and not knowing where you were going?"

"Because when he was in form, I knew that there would be laughing and joking and dancing. The lentils we cooked on a fire were the best meals of my life. There would be wonderful music, even if we made it ourselves, and although he doesn't have a clue about how the world works, somehow he pulled it off, emerged from a soggy trek to a rainbow, from a desert to an oasis. He'd find something new and exciting in the ancient world because he knew where every other scholar and archeologist had looked. Do you know what it's like to be the first people to uncover a three thousand year old rubbish heap?"

***

Before the space is his, Paris takes precise measurements and draws plan after plan of how he envisions his Pythagorean school, picking out features from temples he designed years ago. He had never imagined a Temple of the Muses inside an enclosure, but it all works well. He needs to be as exact and detailed as Isabella, including bathrooms and heating pipes and a coat room. He has to have an inviting and wheelchair-accessible front desk. An architect transposes Paris's drawings into computer-generated blueprints of the overall structure so the work can start. After the shell is complete, he'll select how to use each part of the space.

When he passes papers on the building, using funds from attorney Rothman's office, Paris sets to work with ferocious energy and determination, beginning at dawn and continuing until he's exhausted, then starting again the next dawn. He employs stonemasons, tile layers, carpenters, plumbers, electricians, glaziers, heating and air-conditioning specialists. All study the blueprints on an improvised table. He aims to complete the basic layout in a couple of months and then fill it with objects so that it becomes like a Pythagorean school with a hint of Plato's Academy and Aristotle's Lyceum.

Paris runs to dusty marble yards where diverse colors and sizes of marble and granite slabs lay haphazardly against walls as workers with ear muffs run loud power saws, slicing slabs of rock. The owners walk around the yard with him and present their samples. Paris rubs his fingers on the marble, examines their veins, decides which to buy. He's interested in polished and rough stone, slabs, blocks, and columns.

He takes two hours out of his day to manage his investment portfolio but allows no other distraction or pleasure. Helen has a one-month Fulbright to study and teach in Barcelona, so he doesn't have the distraction of their budding relationship, though he e-mails her regular progress reports. He sleeps little at night, taking short naps in between long stints of high-intensity labor, working with the same obsessive energy as if he were the Emperor Julian the Apostate single-handedly tearing down the dogma of monotheism and restoring the philosophy of Socratic skepticism.

And he commands his workers as they create a dusty,

noisy construction site. They load marble columns and granite slabs from a crane through the large windows. They mark exactly where statues and busts and urns will go and build around them. Movers bring in material, and Paris points them to the right place. Other workers install marble floor tiles, ceiling tiles, wall tiles. Each a different stone. He takes direct charge of every building detail; his demands are not making him a joy with the construction crew, although everyone seems to like being part of the unusual project.

His vision is a product of years of research. Paris's knowledge of antiquity, his exacting eye of what the place should look like, makes the work progress swiftly. Paris learns where to buy material, shipping in items from around the world.

He creates a small living area, isolated with plastic sheeting, in which he has a divan to sleep, a counter he uses as a kitchen, a desk for drawings, and the rudiments of a bathroom. Pretty slim for a millionaire. He will unpack his books and care about his living conditions after he builds the shell.

Lowell drops in on him periodically, seeing the flurry of construction, in some cases giving him a ride to buy more materials.

"I think I understand what you want to do here," he says.

"Pythagoreans were the cutting edge of their age. They saw patterns in the universe, from music to astronomy to mathematics to social interaction. Before them, most people lived without thinking about life."

Lowell cuts short the rant. "Same as today. We live without thinking about the function of the organs keeping us alive."

***

Lowell knows it will be a bad day even before he steps out of bed. He can feel elevated enzymes kicking up his esophagus. Not good. This will lead to prolonged innervation within the gall bladder which would also affect the ancilla in the pancreas.

The best thing would be to keep off carbohydrates all morning, and that's no fun. No bread, no oatmeal, no sugar. But, unusually, he doesn't have an appetite that morning and wonders whether he should check levels of his ghrelin and peptide—two digestive hormones that regulate appetite.

He sees the next sign of a jinxed day out the window in the form of an overcast New England day, full of heavy humidity and opaque frost. This would put stress on the abdominal muscles which would require an increase in blood flow, diverting much needed blood from the small intestine. There's no way around this. He can use a wool sweater to keep his midsection warm, but he can't stop humidity permeating his skin.

Lowell has to take his Irish setter for a walk and suffer. His pee color is up to seven and his stream strength is down to a dangerous three.

Next he sees his daughter's number as his phone starts ringing and he wonders whether he should answer and listen to her chastise him, which seems to be her favorite activity. He can't do anything but appease her, tell her how busy he is, never contradict her. She blames him for scaring off her potential suitors. I mean, how is he supposed to know how squeamish guys are about what muscles are used when you're on the potty?

He doesn't answer the phone.

The next episode of bad news comes from another early morning telephone call. He knows he shouldn't pick up. All his stomach muscles tighten when it rings. He sees the number—Gardner Museum. His mouth goes dry, his kidneys kick. He shouldn't answer when his body is telling him that it's going to be bad news. But the cytoplasm of red blood cells don't take well to procrastination.

Imogen is on the other end of the line.

"Lieutenant Lowell." She gives no greeting, only a harsh voice. He should end the call, pretend that he went out of cell phone range.

But he listens. And it isn't good.

***

Work on Paris's "Temple on a hill" progresses ahead of schedule and starts to look like a majestic Greek temple on top of a building overlooking Boston. In the large open space, floor-to-ceiling columns lead one's vision across the window and over the city. The columns have capitals supporting an elaborate wood ceiling which is reflected in the shiny marble floor. There are places for statues and other objects. One section will be dedicated to music, another to art, and a third to mathematics, the triangle of Pythagorean science. In the center, Paris will put two white classical divans—he sent a design to a furniture maker—with a low granite table between them. He has to build a second floor around the perimeter, making the place like an indoor cloister.

Paris hears the doorbell chime when a worker stops noisily cutting a piece of marble. Another worker pulls marble tiles from a box, and Paris points to the place on the wall where they should go as he walks to open the door. Helen enters looking dejected. Paris is thrilled to see her after two months of his obsessive work and her weeks in Spain. His enthusiasm, the openness and majesty of his Pythagorean school—his future museum—doesn't seem to cheer her.

"A glass of wine?" Paris asks although it's not even midday.

"Please. I'd like that."

"How was Barcelona?"

"It was entirely a working trip."

"You stayed longer than planned."

"I had to advise a new museum."

"It's nice that you're back. You need to advise me too. Let's celebrate properly."

He's thought about her every day, had imaginary conversations with her, preaching Pythagorean philosophy, explaining to her the meaning of his museum, how the ancients lived.

Paris goes to a rough box behind him and pulls out a bottle of 1972 Châteauneuf du Pape and two long-stem glasses that he bought just for her. He uncorks the bottle and pours two glasses. It's a mixture of class and funk, drinking fancy wine in a construction zone.

"What are we celebrating?"

"You here."

They clink and then drink. He sees that she isn't in a celebratory mood.

"This will be a real change for me," he says. "I used to live marginally, drink cheap wine and eat cheap food. But I need to start living and acting urbane."

"You'll do it well. You're naturally classy."

"It's you who gives the place class. I came from a rough neighborhood and wrestled my way up the ladder."

"That's not what class is."

"When you entered just now you interacted with these marble slabs and made them come alive."

"You have the money to fill it with beautiful antiquities."

"I've already started working on that; real antiquities that belong here, not stuff that matches the furniture."

Paris puts his hand on Helen's back to guide her to his first acquisition, a small fresco with the price tag still on it leaning on the wall. She looks at the price.

"Paris, you have to bargain with these people."

"Sixty thousand, fifty thousand—it doesn't worry me. Money begets money. Yesterday alone my investments made forty-eight thousand. I'm on track to make another million before the spring equinox. Besides, I'm a sucker for Apollo-Daphne stuff."

Helen turns away from the art and walks to the center of the large space. She turns and faces Paris. "I've come carrying bad news."

"I can read it in your face. If it's bad news for me, it must be bad for you too since we're partners."

"News that the art has been returned to the museum has somehow surfaced. It will appear in tomorrow's *Globe*."

"What! No one was supposed to know."

"Somehow it leaked. The lieutenant's work is thwarted. Now it will be impossible for him to continue the investigation."

Paris moves around erratically. "Can't we stop them from publishing the story?"

"The *Globe*, yes, probably, but other people know. It'll hit internet gossip. If the *Globe* doesn't publish and legitimize it, someone else will within a couple of days."

"Damn." The import of her words hits him. "Lowell is waiting for D. Jason to return. Now he's sure not to. Did the story include how the art was returned?"

"That part of the story—your identity—hasn't emerged. You're safe."

"I don't care about being safe. I have another reason for not wanting to be known."

"What reason is that?"

Paris begins to calm and sits. "Well, it doesn't matter now, does it?"

Helen too sits. "Lowell feels betrayed. The news must have leaked on our end. His identity wasn't revealed either. He told me that he's going to stay with the case. He wanted to tell you himself, but he let me come first. He said he'll come later to discuss the next step, although now I know there isn't a next step."

"Only a few people knew that the art was returned. Someone among this small group betrayed us. Someone who didn't know Lowell or me."

"Talk has a way of spreading in Boston—an officer at the bank where we withdrew the money chats at a cocktail party with someone who hangs around the museum or the warehouse where we're restoring the art. We couldn't keep a thing like that quiet."

A long silence. Both are looking sadly out the window. Paris can't believe that the leak was a casual mistake.

He says, "I'm really sorry. I wanted you to have your money back. Now I feel terrible about having this money from you."

"No, it's right that you have the reward, especially what you're doing with it. We got back everything that was stolen."

"Almost everything."

"If it hadn't been for you—I mean, if we had to deal with the crooks, they would have wanted two or three times as much."

"We need a new strategy, a new way to get to Tizzio or whoever it is."

"Paris, are you withholding information?"

"You sound like Imogen. She's suspicious by nature, and as much as she wanted the art returned, she hated giving me the money. Now we too have to be suspicious, suspecting who we least expect. Tell me, did any donor have anything to gain from their gifts toward the reward?"

"Absolutely not. Those who donate big money get a plaque on a room, their name in the paper, but these people got nothing. They're the real philanthropists."

"They love art?"

"They're business people who love the museum."

They sit stiff again. He turns off his rational nature, examines his animal instinct, and asks Helen, "Is Dr. Adler known to have a hand in the art underworld?"

"Just the opposite. He's a most respected art dealer with extensive connections. He's both a connoisseur of fine art and an authentication expert."

"An authentication expert," Paris repeats. "I know that."

"Our most enthusiastic trustee. You know that too: he supplied half your reward, and he also raised money for other projects."

"I'd like to meet him. Anonymously, of course. Everyone who studies antiquity knows his name."

"Don't start suspecting powerful people, especially our most loyal patron."

"It seems to me…"

"Don't go there,'" she says. "Let the police do it."

Paris thinks that Lowell can't do anything without him since Paris is now the only link to the thief. They both stand.

"Imogen says that they've done DNA analysis on the crate," Helen says.

"Mine would be the only DNA they'd find. Lowell told me they used the type of pest-treated wood for shipping a crate overseas. The thug never touched it. I gave Lowell my DNA sample."

Paris, thinking, begins walking her to the door. "I wish I'd kept something from D. Jason when he came into the office. I gave into too much rational nature and didn't allow animal instinct. I also wish I had a security camera, but in all the years there I never had even a rumor of a problem. The thieves probably liked my place because I didn't have cameras."

Helen says, "It's been a good partnership. Do we have anything else to discuss?"

Paris, lost in thought, doesn't get the obvious hint. He says, "You said that you have a copy of the Samos vase that's missing."

"A copy."

"I didn't think of this before, but Samos is Pythagoras's hometown. I should have a section dedicated to Samos here. I never before paid much attention to Samos. Yes, we need objects from his youth. Right here in the center of the space. Can I borrow it?"

"It's a copy."

"And you're the only person who knows about it?"

"I saw it a few years ago in the warehouse. I'll dig it out. The real one is the only piece the burglars took that is not famous, unlike the valuable paintings. It will probably appear on the underworld art market."

"It has a new value now. I researched it. It was supposed to be part of a set of four, each based on Aeschylus."

"Yes, a set of four. I thought you detested copies."

"It's all we've got. It's much later than Pythagoras, but we don't have to go into that. His father was a traveling merchant who took his son all around the Mediterranean. Pythagoras went empty, vulnerable, soaking up the learning of every city he visited."

Paris, serious, looks directly at her. "Some people live ordinary lives, and then suddenly the gods demand that they slay the dragon."

"What?"

"Before diving into Hades, we must learn from Orpheus and Eurydice who made the terrible mistake of succumbing to the weak part of their animal nature."

"I guess they were human."

"We're called upon to be heroic. Mystery comes from the Greek 'to close,' as in close your eyes and feel. We're going to open our eyes and erase the mystery."

"Our eyes have been wide open for years and we haven't found a thing."

"I swore an oath of honor to you that you'll have the thief and get your money back. Nowadays no one cares about honor. Leaders give their word then go back on it. It is the antique way to honor your word. This Temple of the Muses is dedicated to the antique way."

She nods but he sees that she doesn't understand.

"Fortuna favors the wise," he adds. "The gods reward those who act."

She moves to the door. He's distracted, doesn't pay attention as she exits. He closes the door and leans on it. Thoughts are firing around his brain. He goes to his computer in the enclosed area, takes off the plastic cover and fires it up. He brings himself a plate of feta and tomatoes and puts it next to his computer. He opens the site for his ancient Greece web community and enters a message, reading aloud as he types:

"Fellow followers of ancient rites: I know that I've been harsh a few times, but no one ever proved my criticism wrong. I desperately need your help to locate three vases from Samos, circa year 150 Before Catastrophe. One of Achilles and Ajax playing dice, another of Persephone picking flowers, and the last of Hercules diving into Hades. They're probably in rough shape, like everything from there. Revelations thankfully accepted. Glory to the gods."

Chapter Eight

Greek philosophers scorned democracy, likening it to mob rule. Read what they said, Paris would tell people who believe that Greece was the cradle of democracy. Democracy condemned Socrates to death. Plato said that the elite—himself and other aristocrats—should rule. They believed that they were naturally superior to the polis and that Greeks were naturally superior to everyone else, who they collectively called *barbarians*, from which we get the word *barba* or *beard*. Greeks were clean-shaven and bathed and everyone else were, well, barbarians.

The philosophers believed that rationality should dominate and that men should free themselves from base emotions and transcend to the realm of reason. This is why women, emotional creatures, are inferior. Men are governed by rationality. A man's sense of honor is rational. A man's sexual desire for women—or boys—is rational, whereas women's desires are animal. War—beating another man on the head with a club—is rational.

When Paris had included those sentences in a criticism of *The Republic*, scholars bombarded him with abusive e-mails accusing him of diverse villainies. Curiously, almost all women saw his irony, his hate mail coming from male professors.

That's what they believed, he wrote back, staying in character.

Paris recalls vividly when he had lost his reason and allowed emotion to dominate, drawing Fortuna's ire. Never again. He must never be hotheaded, must allow the brain time to cool the blood, which Aristotle knew to be the brain's function. One action at a time. Multitasking is a sure way to failure.

He must use his rationality to fulfill his oath to Helen.

Looking in a mirror inside Georgio Armani on Newbury Street, he is forming a strategy. A salesman is fussing over the new suit he's wearing while the house tailor is on his knees marking the cuff. Paris looks up and sees Lieutenant Lowell standing in an archway to protect himself from a late November rain. Paris rushes outside.

"So, you're suddenly becoming a gentleman," Lowell says as Paris steps out. "Fancy clothes. Fancy galas."

"Don't stand in the rain, Lieutenant. No one knows what you're doing, and no one knows my connection to the Gardner art."

They move under a wider awning, the rain splashing at their shoes.

"What's your angle?"

"It's the first step to get close to the thief," Paris says. "I have to be rich."

"You don't have to jargogle anyone—you're already rich."

"I need to look the part. Isabella is my inspiration. I need to *be someone* in Boston, like she was, and I need to do it fast. Our thief must be anxious now, and anxiety makes people stumble. I know that personally."

Lowell says, "I'll be around to keep in touch with you and make sure you'll be all right."

"I guess it means that you'll also be able to keep an eye in case I trip up and show that I was in on the heist."

"Anyone who knows your past would be a fool not to suspect you."

The comment makes Paris take in a deep nasal breath. He says, "The last couple of generations don't know the stories of antiquity, just like those who lived in the Dark Ages were ignorant of them. The stories were moral teachings. Without these stories we have no direction."

"By the way, I like the basic construction of your temple. You really know your stuff."

"I never thought that my years of study would bear practical fruit. But the basic shell of a structure is the beginning. I have to put things inside that the Pythagoreans would have used. Every part of the space has to be carefully thought out. And we can use this place to get closer to our thief. He deals in art, and I need to buy."

"The best way to be a police suspect is to want to help the police. Any investigator would suppose that it was you who leaked the story to the press."

"At least we both suspect that it wasn't leaked by accident."

He runs back in the shop to pay for the suit, and then they both walk under umbrellas to a stuffy, overly neat shop with green leather chairs and pairs of spiffy shoes sitting inside cabinets made from Brazil's rain forest trees. As soon as Paris begins looking, a zealous sales woman approaches and points out different pairs. It seems a game to him, looking and dressing like James Bond. Lowell sits on an armchair, pulls out a wrist gadget and checks his blood pressure.

When they're back outside in the rain, Paris asks Lowell, "Why would I have been part of the heist then stick around and talk to you?"

"Let's go somewhere."

Lowell drives Paris to an unmarked store in Watertown. Inside, high-end security gear is displayed around the spacious room. LED lights are blinking all over. Cameras are turning. Laser beams are searching. A strobe is flashing in the corner. Paris is entranced as soon as he enters.

"You don't want to be another robbery victim like the Gardner Museum," Lowell says. "Your first job is to put security in your place."

Lowell describes the layout of Paris's future museum to the owner.

He replies to Paris, "Museums are easy targets because they're open to the public. You need to install security redundancies—many museums and private homes with valuable art don't have enough security. You need motion detectors and heat sensors to track any activity via fixed video as well as portable cameras. Every door and window has to trigger a sensor. You also need to monitor the outside of the building, and all should be connected to you via an encrypted internet site. That's minimum to start."

"That way the lieutenant will also know every move I make."

"Exactly," Lowell says.

The store owner brings out various components and shows how they work. It's stuff James Bond would find rudimentary but it activates Paris's imagination. Lowell tells Paris to take the entire package.

"Can I have some eavesdropping devices which I can plant?" Paris asks.

The owner shows him pens with cameras, microphones, and transmitters. Finally, he's going to play the master spy—slick, calm, and sophisticated, no longer needing to jump on tables and shoot imaginary arrows at evil enemies.

He buys a tiny microphone that can stick under a desk like chewing gum.

"Cool."

"They have long battery life, but they only transmit a hundred meters."

The owner is happy for the sale.

When they return with the goods to the future museum, Paris says, "My main work is transforming this space into a modern Pythagorean school, an authentic recreation of their world. Like Isabella's museum, everything has to be authentic. Who better to build a Pythagorean school than the person who has meticulously researched them? There's nothing about the ancient world I haven't studied. We don't know much about Pythagoras directly. We have to piece together bits of information and draw conclusions, but I know from experience it will generate interest. "

"From the number of people who bought your book?"

"You can find a book of all existing Greek drama and read them in a couple of days—thirty-four short plays, many incomplete. You can read the histories, the philosophers, the scientists, in a few weeks. You can know all there is to know about ancient literature in a couple of intense semesters because the vast majority of their works were destroyed by monotheists. To know their world we need to study archeologists, anthropologists, linguists, historians, and other scientists. I tramped from one ruin to another."

"Your ex told me."

"I thought she was my Penelope. Her Odysseus failed her, got swept out to sea again." Paris looks around his space. "In Athens and Rome and Alexandria, temples and schools were built outdoors, in the open. But away from the Mediterranean climate, in Boston, it has to be indoors."

"Hippocrates studied the body and its functions, but just about all his conclusions are wrong."

"But he studied. That's the most important contribution Greece gave to the world. Others didn't study."

Lowell looks at the boxes of security equipment. He says that he'll get a techie from the force to help set it up for Paris.

"Continue building," Lowell says. "Live big. Become famous. Better yet, become infamous. Together we'll figure how to trap the thief."

"The board of trustees knew that the art had come back because they were the ones who had to get the money ready. You should investigate each of those people."

"Yeah, the commissioner would be thrilled to hear it. How long do you think he'd stay in his job if he started investigating people like that?"

"There's another strategy we can use: bait the robbers."

"That's what we're doing. You're the bait."

***

After Helen tells Paris the news of the press leak, she returns to her South End corner townhouse. Imogen knocks on the door half an hour later. They're both glum. They sit across from each other in Helen's living room.

Imogen asks, "Have you ever known a classical scholar?"

"Once. He invited me to lunch, and we ended up splitting the bill. I imagine that it would have been a massive insult to a woman in the classical era."

Imogen says, "You think it's a coincidence that Paris knows Dr. Adler?"

"He doesn't know him; he only knows his reputation."

"He's overly concerned about him. And that vase from Samos. Perhaps he's afraid because Dr. Adler has so many contacts, and if Dr. Adler knows Paris, he'd know he's nefarious."

"Perhaps he thinks Dr. Adler could blow his cover. Paris's fear is rational."

Helen notices that her defense of Paris is apparent to Imogen. Helen says, "We must make sure that we don't reveal Paris's identity or we'll be in trouble."

"And I imagine so will Mr. Paris."

"He's entertaining, genuine."

"He's taken a fancy to you."

"We haven't seen each other. I've been away, and he's been busy."

"I'm not sure you want to see him. He's too…too odd, too secretive."

She's made lists of traits she wants in a man. She can't think of any of those traits she would assign to Paris. But as soon as she voiced that he's genuine, she knew it to be true. He has the clear eyes of a person who wants to do good but stumbles over himself in the process.

"He told us how he came across the stolen art," Helen says.

"He knows more than he's telling. You think he took part in the robbery?"

"I can't imagine," Helen says.

"I can. He's too streetwise to be an innocent classical scholar."

"There'll be a line out the door when we announce that the paintings will be displayed."

Imogen stands and thinks out loud, "How does he know that the thief has enough to cover our ten-million-dollar reward? Thousands of stories and tips, but we hadn't gotten anything better than a fake Manet, and not even the right fake. Then out of the blue comes Paris. No, it's too casual."

"Let me get to know him."

"You may be dealing with our enemy. Have you considered that he may have leaked the story to the press to thwart the investigation? We only have his view of events."

When Imogen leaves, Helen walks about her apartment distracted. Here she entertains the big donors of Boston society. She takes out her phone and checks her e-mail and then puts the phone on the marble side table. She takes off her shoes, puts the contract with Paris on the side table. She walks back to the kitchen and turns on the espresso machine to make a decaffeinated latte macchiato. She returns to the living room.

She looks at the paintings hanging on her wall, each lit from a ceiling spot. She has modern sculptures on pedestals from artists she knows. She believes in living in her living room as well as retaining it for show. She picks up the phone and dials.

"Hi, Jenny. I was wondering if you have vacation time coming. I have a feeling that I'll need one soon, not a working trip like I had. Why don't we go after Thanksgiving when it starts getting cold?"

She listens to Jenny listing possible destinations. She also listens to Jenny giving her personal advice.

"You're always trying to fix me up with someone. Let's think about where we can go. I was thinking about Greece. We can see some of the ruins, though the best Greek ruins are outside Greece. I know so little about their art."

She sips her drink. "I don't have a sudden interest in the ancient world." She realizes that she says it too fast. Her friend picks up subtle inflections. "I was just thinking that no one goes to the Mediterranean in winter." She knows that Jenny will ask her more about this the next time they meet. "Let's talk about it later."

She hangs up and picks up a magazine, thumbing the

pages without looking. She puts it down, fidgets with this and that. Then she goes to the side table and picks up Paris's legal contract, skims it, returns it to the table.

"Paris," she says to herself, "I hope you will come through. The museum has been misused too many times before, and so have I."

***

The next day Paris asks Helen to make good on her promise to show him around Boston. Walking with him through Copley Square, Helen points to the public library, the Old South Church, Trinity Cathedral. Paris adores the character of the open square.

"Just like the old days," he says. "The temple next to the agora."

A group of teenagers wearing intentionally ragged clothes are skateboard jumping, looking groovy, passing in front of and behind them. A rugged homeless guy is selling copies of *Spare Change*. Business men and women are walking quickly past. A Duck Tour amphibious vehicle drives down Boylston Street, the driver's microphoned voice telling his tourists tales—some embellished, others dicey—about the square.

As they walk toward the grand public library, Paris delights in the classical bronze statues, representing art and science, which sit on large stone pedestals in front of the Renaissance revival building.

Helen tells him that it's the first free library. "Did the ancient world have free libraries?"

"Of course. Like the famous one in Alexandria which I'm absolutely sure was destroyed by Christians."

"I thought it was Muslims."

"Christians blame them but it was destroyed way before Islam arrived. I researched this thoroughly."

They enter the elaborate edifice, whose lobby has an arched mosaic ceiling, white-and-golden marble dripping with black-and-gray veins, bronze zodiac signs—ancient Greek symbols—inlaid in the marble floor. Paris is spellbound by the classical architecture and imagery as he walks up the grand staircase to the landing. He looks around the open hall which has Sienna marble in between bright frescos of Greek themes: Plato, Babylonian shepherds, nymphs playing with fire, the nine muses rising above Mount Parnassus, Virgil, Aeschylus, and Homer. He stands in awe at the murals. His throat constricts with reverence. In myth, gods have human qualities, human achievement.

"Gods, goddesses—how I missed them while I was confined by Calypso."

Why hadn't he stayed true to his principles? Why had he wrecked his life? The thought makes him nostalgic for when he was a bright young scholar in England, an American finding his way in the English tutor system. He studied under the leading scholars and then went traipsing around the Mediterranean on his own or with Alice to unknown sites.

He sees Helen looking at him; it's a look of compassion. A really well-put-together woman. Independent. She doesn't even know he's Odysseus. Alice loved him dearly, trekked through mud and desert with him, but hers wasn't a compassionate love.

They walk to the next room which has murals of Sir Galahad's quest for the Holy Grail as told by Tennyson.

"History is myth," Paris says. "You can recount ten different stories about the same event."

Helen touches his arm. Her concern makes him feel comfortable. He wants to know who she is, but he can feel that it would be hard for her to open up. He also wants to tell her about his life, but he can't yet.

"This is my art," she says. "Where beauty and daily life intersect."

"New Mexico was my salvation, but also my isolation. I'm ready to rejoin Pythagoras in Croton."

"It will be terrific to have your museum here."

He feels buoyed by her encouragement.

They leave the building and walk down Boylston Street, turning right on Mass. Ave. Helen is telling him snippets of the city's history and how it became a center for art, learning, science, and medicine. They cross the Harvard Bridge, an orange sky encompassing the city. The days are getting shorter. They stop and look over the water between MIT on the Cambridge side and the financial district on the Boston side.

"Art historian and tour guide," Paris says. "You have many talents."

"You could go to any big city and open your museum. Why here?"

"You."

"Me?"

Perhaps he is too direct. "When I saw Athena in the library, I felt as if I had come back to Ithaca after a monster-fighting odyssey. You too are a relic of the ancient world. Doesn't matter how many tech devices you have in your purse, your roots are in ancient customs."

He sees nervousness on her face. As nice as she is, he feels that she has a comfort line no one can cross.

"I've invested half my reward as an endowment," he says. "I'm teaching myself how to trade equities. The rest of the money...I'm planning...Well, I'm inspired by what your founder did."

"Isabella?"

"She did something wonderful with her money. When I was looking at investment opportunities, I stumbled on a list of billionaires. They typically do little for anyone but themselves. Many wouldn't mind giving their workers even less and getting out of paying tax, making them doubly selfish. At least half of them inherited their money. In a sense, I too am inheriting, a gift from the gods, plain old good luck."

"What about you personally?"

"I can attend thousand-dollar-a-plate fund-raisers, become one of those fat cats who gets hit up for donations. You may call me yourself, telling me the advantages of spending fifty thousand dollars for a drinking fountain."

"I can't picture you as a fat cat. But when I do ask for

a donation, I hope you'll be generous."

"You'd be hard to resist."

Paris checks himself—another too blunt comment. They turn and resume walking over the Charles River toward Cambridge.

"Maybe you'll put a plaque with my name near one of the paintings that I returned."

"And what name would that be?" She stops walking. "I forgot—I'm not supposed to know."

"A hero has a divine birth but never a childhood. A hero must never doubt the outcome."

"It's good to doubt yourself," Helen says.

"I doubt myself all the time. That's why I'm always right."

She smiles at the statement, both playing and true. "At least tell me why you left academia."

"Oh that. Circumstances. The gods get upset when a mortal becomes too powerful. Anyway, my kind is evolving to extinction. I taught three classics classes a year, and one had to be an overview. A couple of graduate students a year. The rest of the time they wanted me to teach things like early Chinese dynasties."

"You retreated into your world? Perhaps there's a middle ground."

"No there isn't. Water things down and you end up wet and empty."

"You should learn to compromise."

"You mean I'm dogmatic?" He smiles mischievously. "I had to make a change, leave town. Paris was a baby left exposed on a mountaintop because the Queen of Troy dreamed that a child would set fire to Troy. But he was rescued by a shepherd. It's an allegory for being rescued here, ready to set the town on fire. What's your life story?"

"I began working at the Gardner museum a few years ago."

"Did you have anything to do with the investigation of the theft?"

"Not until you approached me. Imogen worked on the theft. She wanted the art returned. Now she wants the thief punished." She turns serious. "Paris, do you know who it is?"

"If I did, I'd tell Lowell."

"But you suspect."

"I think the thug's boss lives here in Boston; maybe we passed him walking down the street. Lowell has the tools to track him down. Like Oedipus, he must solve the riddle of the Sphinx."

"There's something else, isn't there?"

"I don't know. One thing doesn't fit: the missing vase."

"It didn't physically fit with the paintings. Or perhaps it got lost or broken. It doesn't have value compared to the paintings."

Paris is silent. Everything is right about Helen but something isn't right about that vase. Why was it stolen in the first place? Just then Paris thinks that he needs his friend Barry's help.

Paris puts his hand on the small of Helen's back but then timidly pulls away. They look at each other. Paris is the first to look away. Students with backpacks are walking around them. A trailer parked on the street is selling falafel sandwiches.

"It's easier when you don't have to reveal yourself," she says.

"By Hercules! You reveal more than you think."

"So do you."

He sees the Greek pillars in front of MIT's Infinite Corridor. He points toward the corridor. "We're always trying to return to their world."

***

Isabella Stewart Gardner was a talked-about woman. Anyone with a tongue for scandal followed her every provocation, from smoking in public to brandishing large hats during Boston Symphony Orchestra performances. They talked about every male she bumped into, and she bumped into many. She wore French fashion, exposing more flesh than Boston puritans were accustomed to. Even noncontroversial acts fanned the flames of story. She did nothing to quell the rumors about her, adding witty one-liners which appeared with exclamation points in newspaper gossip columns. Henry James cast her life in *Portrait of a Lady*.

Paris has been studying Isabella's life since the night he opened D. Jason's locker. She took a complete hands-on approach to designing, building, and running her villa/museum, and was seen dressed in work clothes, mixing mortar and hammering support beams. She was both fun and frustrating to work for, selecting every piece of art and its location, engrossing herself in every detail, from grand paintings to ivory letter openers. She intended her decisions to last forever, which is no small amount of time.

She and the museum directors who followed lived on the top floor of the villa, operating all aspects of fund-raising, human resources, publicity, and running the museum. Everyone moved to larger quarters when it got too crowded, which was shortly before the museum was robbed, so no one was around to hear the racket the robbers were making or to keep the night guards under check. Paris will live in his museum just as Isabella lived in her villa.

Paris is entranced by her remedy for misfortune, the way she transformed a piece of empty land into one of the most aesthetically pleasing places in America and shared her vision with the world. She embraced the same aesthetics as Pythagoras, becoming a guiding light for what Paris wants to achieve.

When Paris is not up late at night reading about candlestick charts, Fibonacci retracement, Bollinger Bands, and other investment tools, he's reading about Isabella and using her model for his museum.

Paris begins feeling confident researching investments. It involves the same principles as researching the ancient world. First, don't take just one person's word no matter how authoritative. Second, investigate from different angles. Third, never let animal emotion cloud your work or it will destroy your judgment. Successful investing requires rational nature, Pythagoras's dispassionate world of numbers. Ironically, money, which meant nothing to the Pythagoreans since they lived communally, is Paris's modern vehicle for presenting them.

***

Lieutenant Lowell is not the typical visitor Helen shows around the museum. Her usual guest is somewhere between an art connoisseur and an art expert. Those who wish to expand their knowledge of art go with one of the docent-led tours which examine the basic collection, concentrating on a dozen pieces that exemplify periods and styles. Helen usually has the privilege of showing the museum to the real art lover—or more precisely, the real art lover has the privilege of being shown around the museum by Helen. She not only knows facts but bubbles with enthusiasm when talking about a painting or artist. And she doesn't confine herself to the museum: she talks about the beauty of dashes on the road for pedestrian crossings, telephone poles, curvy freeway exchanges and sewer grates—whatever comes from human hands and human imagination.

The lieutenant had contacted Helen and announced his desire to start his art education at the Gardner. Yes, he told Helen, it would be his first time there. "Well, more like Art 102. I've been to the Louvre."

When Helen meets him in the modern glass-front lobby, he pulls back his shoulders and pulls in his stomach.

"Your brain shrinks half a percent a year after you hit sixty," Lowell says without introduction. "And you start asking yourself, what's it all about? You think about that?"

"I haven't yet hit forty."

"I mean, I'm not saying that you look sixty."

He snatches a look to see if she's offended. He's not sure.

"I mean, you look pretty good for a gal of forty."

They cross an enclosed walkway to Isabella's Italianate villa. Helen's friendliness puts him at ease. He has to pay attention not to make another faux pas. Yes, he tells her, he has an idea that art has eras. Then he says, "Eras. About how long would each era be?"

The for-instance she gives is that Rembrandt and Vermeer lived at the same time and in the same country. He knows about the Vermeer and three Rembrandts that were stolen because he studied each piece. He knows that Vermeer's *The Concert* is one of the most valuable pieces ever stolen, second only to the *Mona Lisa*.

They stop in front of John Singer Sargent's *El Jaleo*, a large, dark, flamenco scene of a Gypsy dancing in front of musicians. "Sargent was a friend of Isabella's," she tells him.

Helen escorts Lowell to the courtyard surrounded by a cloister-like passage. The large skylight covering the courtyard makes the space open and bright. Helen tells him that Isabella's building was influenced by the Palazzo Barbaro in Venice. He hears a fountain. The floor in the center is an old Roman black-and-white mosaic surrounded by ancient statues and dozens of plants and flowers. A big ancient jug lies on its side. Lowell looks up and notices four stories of columns and arches, all open to the light of the patio they are standing in. He is struck by its handsomeness and the peace the space creates.

"Many museums begin as institutions sponsored by the government," Helen says, "such as the Museum of Fine Arts down the road, the Metropolitan in New York, the Art Institute in Chicago, the Louvre.

"The Louvre. Like I said, I've been there and seen how they act in front of the Mona Lisa."

"Other museums begin as private collections."

"You're talking about collections of the rich."

"Of course rich, to be able to afford both the art and the building. The National Gallery in Washington began as Andrew Mellon's private collection."

"Did he know art?"

"He was a businessman. He got swindled a few times, spending millions on what turned out to be fraudulent items, but he also collected wonderful pieces."

"It seems to me that people like him contribute to the country, but they make art a business."

"Wise observation." The compliment gives Lowell confidence.

Lowell is at heart a liberal. He doesn't like the type of rich who not only buy yachts but also buy people. Policemen see the underclass of society, those used and abused by the powerful. One thing Lowell has learned during his years on the force: put a normal person in a bad neighborhood—a poor school, a challenged family—and you have a good chance of turning him into a criminal.

Helen says, "One person's trash is another person's art."

That's exactly what Lowell said to himself earlier. They walk among the friezes and sarcophagi around the courtyard. Everything looks old and mismatched. The courtyard has different types of columns for each window, different capitals on each column, different tiles on floors and walls, and they seem grubby and stained. The crisp homogeneity of an ideal American house is absent, lacking what Lowell aims for in his house, fresh and symmetrical. He thinks of how he trims his lawn and keeps his front stairs polished.

Helen points out features of Isabella's villa. Lowell is a skilled listener, asking questions about everything. She seems amused to lead a novice among what he calls "old stuff."

"America didn't have its own art until the late 1800s. We're a working country; our job takes precedence over family and friends. Even if we have all the money we need, we still devote our lives to making more."

Lowell figures that she also gives that explanation to her rich friends. She leads him up the stairs that all visitors use, the same stairs the robbers used. They are greeted on the next floor by tapestries. Lowell asks when they were made, if they used different color threads or dyed them when they were finished, if they were woven by hand or by children.

They go through the Early Italian Room and the Raphael Room, which has a small Raphael *Pietá* and Botticelli's colorful *Tragedy of Lucretia.* The rooms have ornate fireplaces. Light floods in from the courtyard. Lowell concentrates on the volume of religious art, one crucifix followed by a Madonna-and-child followed by portrayals of Biblical stories.

"That's what people knew," Helen says. "Just as we know stories about the Beatles and Neil Armstrong stepping onto the moon. They painted what they knew, each artist putting his spin on it."

"Why are there naked bodies in paintings about Jesus?"

"See how the people in the paintings come out of the canvas. You feel their personalities. You almost feel the fabric of their clothes. Stand and look and you'll feel the story behind the scenery."

"But the naked bodies?"

"And notice that they have more pounds here and there and are not the perfect bodies you see today in *Vogue.* Artists show us intimacy. If they just drew bodies, it wouldn't be art. The artist adds feelings and interpretations."

"The men look muscular and so do the women."

"Being plump was a mark of privilege. They depicted the body while we idealize it."

Lowell is happy to hear that. He thinks how he would draw the human body. Artists look on the outside—the skin, the eyes. They ignore the visual cortex in the back of the brain, and the visual cortex cannot function without the heart pumping oxygenated blood to it, and the heart needs the lungs to oxygenate, and the wind pipe and the...All is fed by digestion, a complete system. Artists pay no attention to organs. They paint skin.

Lowell sees many of Isabella's family portraits in the Short Gallery. He notices that she was a handsome but not beautiful woman. When a woman knows she isn't pretty, it frees her to pursue her interests.

Each room in the museum has its own silence. They enter the Tapestry Room, a room as big as Lowell's house. In the Dutch Room he sees the empty frames of the robbed paintings. He sees the ornate ceilings on the third floor, examines *Europa* in the Titan Room, which he knows to be the most valuable work of art in the building. They come to what looks like a complete church with kneelers in front of stained glass of the saints.

Chapter Nine

Paris's friend Barry steps out of terminal *B* at Logan with a suitcase. A chauffeur-driven black car pulls up. Paris waves to get Barry's attention. They approach each other with warm greetings. The driver puts the suitcase in the trunk.

"It's really nice of you to bring me out here," Barry says. "We've got to wait a bit until the sale papers come through for the storage business. The guy wants to close before the end of the year. You sure you want to give me that much money for handling it?"

"It's only a sliver."

"I'm making it so that no one can trace you. Except that thug D. Jason—who, I guess, knows you by sight."

Paris opens the car door. Barry climbs in.

"Lowell told my ex-probation officer to guard my identity. The police are still monitoring the storage unit."

"No one can tell," Barry says. "Not even the girl working there."

That evening, Paris takes Barry to dine at the Fairmont Copley Plaza, a stuffy, old-money establishment. The waiters have worked there since the Great Depression. Paris is wearing his Armani suit. He gave Barry a suit, which he wears uncomfortably.

"I can see living like this," Barry says as their entrée arrives.

"I'm doing this for a purpose. That table with the two robust gentlemen. They deal in art. We're trying to get known here."

Barry gives a sideways glance then turns back to Paris. "I haven't been able to get any more info on the car break-in where Jason's license was stolen. But I noticed two things that might interest you. The names you sent me."

"The Board of Trustees."

"One guy is also on the board of the car rental company. He's an art connoisseur."

"They're all art connoisseurs since they're on an art museum board."

"There's nothing else interesting about any of them except they're rich and have their names on various companies."

"None of them know Lowell or my identity. The story got leaked to the press without that information. What did you find about Ernesto Adler?"

"He isn't the biggest fish in that pool, but he's been there as long as the director."

"He's our target. Very knowledgeable, expert on the classical period. Good eye for art. Rational nature would never suspect him, but animal nature says otherwise. Can you find his net worth?"

"Already checked. Estimated at fifty million. That means he shelled out a tenth of his empire to you, which shows how desperate he was to get the paintings. What do you know about him?"

"No one quite knows his past," Paris says. "He does nothing to erase the mystery. There are bits of gossip about South America and Germany, educated in Europe, polyglot, expert in ancient art but also deals in modern, specializing in rare and expensive pieces for select clients—private collectors and institutions. He's rich, aristocratic, cultured, a dark handsome gallant man from the old school. He has a gallery on Newbury Street in Boston and another in the Chelsea art district of New York, but they represent a minor part of his empire. Most deals are probably done over the phone from his chic apartment while he's in his silk robe. He's known for his philanthropy to the arts, his sophistication, his personal connections, his enthusiasm for promoting new talent."

"Do I sense envy? Why are you focusing on him?"

"I can't explain it rationally. There's something else besides envy."

"You want us both to put everything on the line for a

hunch?"

"Only if you want to."

"Might be a fun ride, but if you're wrong?"

Paris has thought about this. "I'll be ruined."

The waiter takes away plates. Paris sees the two gentlemen in the neighboring table periodically looking over his way. He orders two chocolate mousses and two Grand Marnier. The waiter nods and goes.

Paris says, "I already contacted someone saying that a millionaire is ready to spend big bucks on artifacts from southern Italy. He'll tell Dr. Adler, and then I'll arrange a chance encounter."

"The cop they have on the case is good. He's solved a lot of other heists."

"Lieutenant Lowell," Paris says. "At first sight he looks like a clumsy oaf. He's really interested in digestion. Now I would never underestimate him. He knows every move I make. What's the second thing you noticed?"

"The FBI has a national list of people related to forged and stolen art."

"Of course, I'm on that list."

Barry nods, pauses, looks at Paris. "That should make you their prime suspect."

"Achilles had to choose between a long and happy life or *kleos*, a short life of glory."

"The cops would have to think that you could have been part of the art underworld all along and made up a story of finding the paintings, waiting just the right time, until your parole expired, to return them."

"That's what you and I have to do now, delve into the underworld and rely on Lowell. I have to start making forgeries again. We need to buy and sell, get known in the business, like with those two over there." Paris points with his eyes. "I have to make an impact in Boston as a rich art buyer, a chump who doesn't care where the pieces come from. We have to deal with slime bags. I'm supposed to lure in the thief, and Lowell is supposed to nab him."

"And you want me to help you buy and sell?"

"The antiquities forgery business is our path to the thief."

"Sounds dangerous, given your prior."

"One of them I have to buy myself for an astronomical sum."

"Let me get this straight: you're going to make a phony piece of art."

"An antiquity."

"Then you're going to offer big bucks."

"Millions."

"To buy back this forgery."

"But the secret is that it will pass through an intermediary."

"Who will want his share of big bucks."

"Millions. Think it will work?"

***

Many people romanticize the old days. Paris does not. Life was truly tough back when men labored dawn to dusk and women even longer. Death was a daily presence: the death of children, the death of mothers, death from malnutrition, war—and there was always war—death from minor infections, malaria, dysentery, the pox. The importance of sanitation wasn't understood. Medical knowledge was mostly erroneous. And every tribe was an enemy of every other.

If it didn't rain in spring, a family might have to kill their newborn so the family could survive. If a boy cut himself, and it became infected, that was it—no second chance. Childbirth, the most hazardous activity, worse than war, killed one in four women, mostly during their first birth—girls, thirteen or fifteen, whose hips had not evolved as fast as human heads had enlarged. Every girl had children. If she didn't by the time she was nineteen, as much as she tried, she was dismissed as having shrugged off her communal duty and would live as shamed as men who hadn't been in war, even if there was no war.

The ancients lived in a world of ghosts and magic, amulets and spells. An entire class of people read signs and talked to spirits, from oracles to auguries who interpreted sacrificed animal entrails.

Paris has studied the four Bronze Age civilizations, all of which appeared about five thousand years ago. Along the Nile, the Euphrates, the Ganges, and the Yangtze, humans began building dwellings, harvesting crops, and domesticating animals. Later the Greeks and Romans invented philosophy and what we now call the scientific method, and this is what Paris celebrates.

Before his downfall, Paris wrote about the importance of retaining an attitude of discovery rather than one of dogma and repression. The monotheists, Paris wrote, think that they destroyed mythology, but what they did was destroy science and replace it with mythology.

The setting sun envelopes the city in an orange glow that radiates over Paris's marble columns as if it were a majestic villa overlooking the Mediterranean. Paris, screw gun in hand, is on a ladder securing a granite slab while singing along to Strauss's opera *Electra*, his voice reverberating off the stone walls. He's alone, finishing a wall, the end of the first phase of construction. His mind is plotting each move he has to make to catch the thief. The doorbell chimes, and he climbs down to answer.

Helen enters wearing casual Patagonia and is rightly amazed by the magnificence of his project.

"Wow." She walks around. "Wonderful. Terrific."

It lifts Paris's spirit to hear those words from someone with such a high aesthetic sense. She was too depressed to look around when she came last time to tell Paris about the news leak.

"The basic structure is almost done," Paris says. "Two solid months of intense work. Now the real work starts, making the place like the Pythagorean commune. This will take many months. Let me show you around. I need your artistic advice."

He brings Helen into the central section. "You'll be

happy to know that Pythagoras practiced equality of the sexes, starting with his wife."

"So different from the Athenians."

"It's my observation that when a society has a hard life, men dominate more severely. In Egypt, which was rich and fertile, they had a lot more sexual equality than did the desert tribes. The Pythagoreans lived in relatively lush Italy while the Greeks and Middle Easterners lived on the edge and needed the strength of patriarchy. It's been shown that shepherds have that hard culture of honor and shame much more than agrarian societies—honor revolves entirely around sexuality."

"I hope you'll present that idea here."

If she was trying to interrupt a rant, he didn't notice.

"This will be the most accurate museum re-creation of ancient life ever. No reason for me to be humble. It isn't a frilly thing for tourists. Other restorations like Kronos in Crete are full of errors. Most people get their vision of ancient life from those ridiculous Hollywood productions. Everything is wrong. The actors wear clean ironed robes, which in real life might have been their only garments, and everyone is well fed and sandaled. Many have muscles that come from working out on a Nautilus. They're well shaven and groomed. The women are tall and blonde—either warriors or Virgin Marys—not busy taking care of nine dirty children."

"I can see that you are indeed inspired by Isabella."

He gets the hint that he should stop, but he still has a couple of things to say.

"Isabella was like Pythagoras. They both wanted us to be surrounded by art and music. The Pythagoreans built and adorned with ideal geometric shapes. They imbued their architecture with balance, what the Chinese call fêng shui."

That's enough of a speech for now.

"I bought another piece of art," he says.

He leads Helen to a frieze of a wrestling scene from classical mythology.

"It's from near Croton at the boot of Italy where the

Pythagoreans had their commune. But this piece is much later than his era."

"And you got this through a retail dealer?"

"I know I paid too much, but the artist gives us everything: plants, architecture, the position of the wrestlers. It's almost as if he made this for future generations to see how they lived. That makes it valuable to someone who wants to show how they lived."

"How do you know it's real?"

"Nobody knows this stuff better than I do."

Perhaps he should add, he and Dr. Adler. He ushers Helen to the triangle center of the room.

"Pythagoras's sacred symbol," Paris says.

Helen sits on a wooden box, the Boston skyline visible outside the window.

Paris points to the setting sun. "The ancients faced their temples like this to let the morning sun sweep through the door and chase away the demons of the night. Atreus made the sun rise in the west."

"Beautiful."

"You make this place beautiful."

"A born gentleman. Or maybe it's hero more than gentleman?"

Her humor flattens him. He reins himself in. Is he going to let her down like he let down Alice? "I'm more of an anti-hero. My past is a pretty big disappointment as a hero."

"To make a new start you have to leave your past behind."

"I used to teach a research methods class. It was one of those classes that students hate. Never trust anyone, I told them. Suspect every source, every testimony. That doesn't work for relationships."

"Paris, you're learned and expressive in certain areas. No one would doubt your authority on the classical world."

"But I don't understand people."

"And you never will since you're so stubborn."

"Stubborn. That's another quality I stressed in that

class: keep at it even if no one believes you."

***

Dr. Adler is pacing around Helen's office.

"How could the information have gotten out?" he asks.

"We tried to be so careful, allowing only a small number of people to know. Perhaps we shouldn't have started restoration work since it involved others. No one knows how this secret could have gotten out."

"Who is the policeman in charge?"

Helen starts to say, then checks herself. She can't give away that information however trustworthy Dr. Adler is. Perhaps she should suggest to Lowell that he involve Dr. Adler since he has so many contacts in the art world and has made it his life's work to investigate the theft.

"I believe Imogen works directly with the police commissioner." She's satisfied with her diplomatic response.

"There's no chance that the police will uncover a trace?"

"Imogen gave me little hope. She felt bad for the police because they warned us to be careful and not leak the information. One of us must have unwittingly betrayed them. We're back to where we were before, except that now we have the art."

Adler calms down and sits. "On the contrary," he says, "the thief should now be easy to catch."

"Why? How?"

"The person who returned the art—"

"He doesn't know. I mean, the police say that he doesn't know."

"Who is he?"

"No one knows. It's in the contract that his identity has to be kept secret. We went out of our way to make sure we remain ignorant, otherwise it would cost us another ten million, which you know we don't have. We don't want to know who he is lest, heaven forbid, that information gets out as well."

"But the ten million we gave him—that should be easy to trace. Where did he put the money?"

"We don't want to know, do we? It might put us in real trouble. We should look elsewhere. If we make another mistake, it will come back and hurt us. The thief, the police think, is very far away."

"No, no. The most successful thief is always right under your nose. That's the only way you can be a good thief. At least that's what thieves say."

"I can't imagine you know anything about thieves."

Gentleman's chuckle, rich man's bow. "A real thief, Ms. Muller, will be the lucky man who steals your heart."

"Maybe that's been my mistake. I've been trying to give it away rather than have someone steal it."

***

Paris, dressed in his designer casuals, is sitting at one of the long oak tables in the Bates Hall Reading Room of the Boston Public Library engrossed in a book. Statues stand between bookcases in the stately room. Next to him on the table sit a laptop and two other open books. He stops reading, puts his fingers on the laptop's keyboard and types a few words, then begins reading again. A green-smocked assistant walks toward him carrying a few books with call slips sticking out. The assistant stops behind Paris and puts down two books, *Who's Who in Boston 1990* and *Successful 19th Century Art Forgeries*. Then the assistant looks at another slip.

"We have to go to another area to dig this up."

Paris looks up, and the assistant shows him the slip. "I've got lots to keep me busy."

"I don't think anyone has ever paged this book, certainly not since we got rid of our card catalog and went on computers thirty years ago."

"That's what every book lover dreams about, a chance of finding something no one else has seen."

The assistant leaves, and Paris continues studying late into the night. The lights are on and Paris is still studying when an announcement over the public address says that the library will close in fifteen minutes. Three or four other people put their papers together and leave. Paris too wipes his brow, closes his laptop and puts it in its case. The assistant passes with a cart. Paris hands his books to him and leaves the large echoing hall.

While passing the mural of Athena, Paris looks up at her. "Good night Gray-Eyed Goddess. Please nudge the thief into our web."

Lost in thought, he descends the ample marble stairs guarded by stone lions and leaves the library. A homeless guy approaches for spare change, and Paris reaches in his pocket and pulls out a ten. He walks past the Old South Church to Newbury Street and turns left. He continues to Adler's art gallery and sees a sales clerk closing the door and locking it.

Winter has come to Boston, the trees bare, the wind ice cold, the streets full of salt and sand from the last snow. He walks up to her. "Excuse me, does Dr. Adler ever come to the gallery?"

"Not usually, but he's been in town a lot recently, and he'll be taking care of the gallery off and on next week because we're getting a new exhibit."

He thanks her and walks off. Two drunks in business suits bump into him and make a lot of noise walking down the street. Paris, disgusted, brushes off his arm.

***

Lying in bed the next morning, Paris is thinking of his philosophical treatise, "What Use is History?" After the success of his lively book on the Pythagorean community in Croton, his publisher pushed for another popular work. They didn't care about his disgrace; they even thought that a prison record would spike sales. Here was the man who fooled the world. But Paris was too broken, too unsure of what to do, so he waited. He waited and he thought.

Now is his time to end dispassionate philosophy and begin action. He must use both Pythagoras's rational nature and Odysseus's warrior instinct. He needs to focus on what he wants his new building to represent. The Pythagoreans lived their religion, not kept it in a temple. He needs to pinpoint the main ideas and mold them into a detailed mission statement. He wants to show the Pythagorean system of thinking and living, to inspire new Pythagoreans, remaining open to however the structure evolves over the years.

He's thinking that Pythagoras lived around the time of Buddha. Although thousands of miles apart, they both broke away from their privileged lives and experienced trials, Buddha practicing extreme ascetics and Pythagoras dashing around the Mediterranean seeking wisdom. Travel was no holiday. He was almost sold into slavery and often threatened with death by starvation, shipwreck, and robbery.

The communities he founded share many of Buddha's practices, including times of silence and contemplation. They both taught freedom through proper living, believing that the cosmos is ordered and harmonious; it's an upbeat message, as opposed to monotheists who have, almost by definition, a stark black-or-white world. Buddha and Pythagoras did not separate spirit and body. They taught the middle path: shying away from war and extremism.

Paris began presenting this to the world in his book; now he is ready to show it.

Around midday, Paris is strolling down Massachusetts Avenue in front of Harvard University. Students and professors are going in and out of Harvard Yard, reminding him of his time in academia. Looking on as an outsider, it feels like a world isolated from life's hard knocks. Academics do not take up arms against others; they live in rational nature. That is what made his break-in to destroy the evidence that would have exposed his Navarite hoax way outside accepted behavior and led to his absolute disgrace.

His destiny is now determined. The gods are calling him to reintroduce Pythagoras, the man who united science and religion, math and art. First, he has sworn an oath to bring the thief out of the underground so Lowell can nab him.

He walks up to Karnak Books, a dark, musty rare bookstore on the second floor of a building that should have been torn down decades ago. Shelves of old books reach up to the ceiling and piles of books sit on the floor. Paris stands in front of a wall of classics. He knows almost every book there but pulls down a few titles and examines them. He takes his purchase of six books to the counter where the bookseller has the face of a nerdish scholar as ancient as his books.

"Did you find what you're looking for?"

"This is as good as Charring Cross Road. I've been buying from you online, but it's so much better to look at the shelves."

Paris is thinking that in a few years, such places, now rare, will be extinct.

The bookseller turns the books on their spines and looks at the titles.

"You should come often. We get a lot of people who read classics, so our stock changes. But some books are rare and expensive."

"I just moved here; let me leave my e-mail address. When you get a rare Golden Age classic, please write me."

"Surprising how in our modern world the number of people interested in classics remains steady."

"Walking around Harvard, it's hard to ignore the Greek influence, from the architecture of the buildings to the style of learning. The biggest contribution the Greeks made was a method of learning. Pythagoras started it. Socrates, Plato, and Aristotle came later with many others whose work has been lost in between. Their method led us to the Internet, the space station, modern medicine.

"Every few centuries fundamentalists gain power. They have an answer to everything, replacing query with dogma, science with suppression. They can't tolerate learning. They try to erase our heritage, destroy our past. They're always telling everyone else how to live. They shut down new ideas, subjugate women, outlaw music, dance, and theater. The Greeks viewed belief as a monstrously low level of philosophy, but today that monster remains a powerful force inside our society. It's linked to masculine authoritarianism, and it plunges society into a dark age, as it did when the Roman Empire came under the rule of the Church."

The bookseller listens with slight interest. Paris's rant is solidifying his own thoughts about what he wants his neo-Pythagorean school to represent. Yes, Paris thinks, he wants it to celebrate free thinking. However rough a life the ancients had, their philosophy was celebratory while the monotheists institutionalized grief, guilt, and shame.

The bookseller looks at one of the titles and adds his own wrath against modernity. "You can find this as an e-book. You can see the words, but you can't experience it except from real books."

"I guess to be completely real, we should be looking at papyrus scrolls."

"I've never touched papyrus. Scrolls don't exist anymore. Outside clay and stone, the ancient world has hardly left a physical trace."

Paris is thinking about how building his Pythagorean museum can draw out the Samos vase. He needs more research. He needs to talk to Lowell.

***

Lowell is in Brigham and Women's Hospital when Paris phones. Not that there is anything wrong with the lieutenant; he just needs to check if the alkalinity levels inside his colon fluctuated during the past week. He is studying whether eating certain grains counteracts methane that builds up in that part of the body, methane being a byproduct of excess alkalinity. He notices the few times he comes on the scene of a homicide that the first parts of the skin to discolor are at the beginning and end of the large intestine, which informs him of the sensitivity of those parts to the slightest deviation in blood flow. His colon pH level is definitely something to worry about.

"Our modern lifestyle puts tremendous chemical stress on the sigmoid colon," he tells Paris.

Paris, in the back seat of a black livery car, picks up Lowell at the hospital entrance. They drive to the restaurant Troquet, taking a table overlooking the Public Garden.

Paris says, "I've been reading about the Boston art world. It's hard to get to the bottom of things, but I wanted to get your opinion."

Lowell says that they should study the menu. "Don't order shellfish; on cold days it breaks down differently in the duodenum lining." He gives Paris a five-minute lecture about how proteins separate before reaching the small intestine, advising him to order rice rather than wheat as a carbohydrate. Except bread. "If you don't have bread with a meal, you don't have a meal."

"The Pythagoreans were vegetarians," Paris says. "People say they also stayed away from beans, but that was an Aristophanes joke."

"Beans and alkalinity, an explosive subject."

Countless stories about the Pythagoreans exist, many preposterous and contradictory, but Paris meticulously researched each rumor from playwrights, historians, and philosophers, combed both archeological evidence and extant personal accounts, and arrived at a good idea of what their commune was like.

"One thing I can't find any info about is Tizzio. Who is he?"

"Big time crook. He's thought to have coke offices in Bogotá and Mexico City, protecting young girls in Bangkok, diamonds in Angola, but all those allegations may be a diversion he created."

"Why don't you arrest him?"

"No one knows anything about him. His people have a buffer; they don't know who they work for. One of his guys designs an operation and gives the information to a second guy who hires the burglars. The second guy skips town, so if the burglars are caught and meet the design guy, they wouldn't recognize him. Tizzio has always been a step ahead of us. The commissioner thinks he buys dirty cops through an intermediary because he keeps getting inside information."

"He's American?"

"Probably. He doesn't seem to come up for air. People

hire him to get a specific piece of art. He's been involved in robbing antiquities in unstable countries like Iraq. The guy is good at what he does."

"You think he's an art connoisseur?"

"Probably not."

"But he's after art."

"Problem is, when people steal this type of thing, they don't have much of a plan in their noggin. They rob a museum, thinking the paintings are worth a fortune. But then they can't do anything with them except look at them, but they're not arty-farty types, so they don't even get a kick in their pants from that. What they robbed becomes a pain in the gazoo."

"Maybe someone hired him for the Gardner heist. Why do you think the thieves held on to the art instead of turning it in for the reward?"

"Fear. Disorganization. Maybe the art got turned over from one crook to another. In the United States it's illegal to pay a ransom. Everyone does it, but when police are involved, they limit bargaining."

"So it's better not to involve the police?"

"It's better to do what is most efficient. We're not allowed to reward a thief; that would encourage thievery. We've been trying to tap Tizzio's investment empire." Lowell sips water, swishing it around to make sure it isn't cold when going down his esophagus. "The prudent policeman would assume that *you're* connected to Tizzio."

"You're not supposed to know too much about me."

Lowell laughs from his stomach.

"Do you know I was a high school punk?"

"One fingerprint is all it takes to get someone's file—when they had measles to what type of shoelaces they use. Your file isn't pretty, especially when it comes to art."

"Please don't tell Helen." Paris takes a change-the-subject breath. "I think there's a more important investment empire to go after: Dr. Adler."

"He's been looking for the art for years, posting a big reward. How can that make him the thief?"

"Remember what you said about the best way to become a police suspect? You go out of your way to help the police."

"I worry about you contacting Adler."

The waiter brings bread and takes their order. Lowell spends a few minutes explaining how he wants his rice cooked. The waiter is especially polite, bestowing good wishes as he heads to the kitchen.

"It's weird having more money than others" Paris says. "You can get others to do anything—serve you dinner, clean your clothes—just by paying them. They'd never serve you dinner otherwise, but if you pay, they work hard and serve you that meal as if you're doing them a favor, falling all over themselves, asking if you're happy, if there's anything else they can do. Just because of money. Rich people get others to stand all day selling products they themselves don't believe in. In older times the rich paid the indigent to build fences that took away their own property. And they're real solicitous to the rich while doing it. All you do is give them money."

As he's saying this he's thinking that he has to use his new wealth to leverage Adler into an inferior position.

Lowell says, "Money doesn't grow from the ground like tomatoes. Some people sweat, others sit behind a desk, but no one *makes* money; we pass it around from person to person."

"When people realize they're old, they start hoarding."

"My wife, she's been hoarding for a long time."

Paris looks around the restaurant at the upper class diners. "I swore an oath to Helen that I would find the thief and return the museum's money."

"Where will you find the thief? You won't have much luck through D. Jason."

"Lieutenant, we need both our talents. I know how to research, and my specialty is the ancient world. The missing vase is part of my expertise. I feel it can solve the crime. I think the thief—not the burglars, but the one who commands—knows something about art. They stole the Samos vase. The thief is on to something."

"Why are you so interested in that vase?"

"Honestly, Lieutenant, I don't know, except that there's something fishy about it. My animal nature feels it's connected to Adler. Let's suppose, as you suggest, that the art I stumbled on in New Mexico got out of the original thieves' control."

"Like someone in Tizzio's organization turned against him and took the art for himself? I doubt it. First of all, they couldn't fence it. The only thing you can do is use it to get out of jail, like in Monopoly. Second, I imagine that stealing something that belongs to Tizzio would reduce your life-expectancy."

"Something is out of control. Perhaps the art is out of Tizzio's control."

"Hunting after Tizzio won't lead to anything but frustration. Art crime has increased dramatically. It's now a six-billion-dollar business, right behind drugs and guns, as the most lucrative international organized crime activity. Those syndicates use the same criminal network they use for human trafficking to transfer stolen art around the world. Terrorist cells fund their activities through stolen art. But the art they rob isn't high-end—it's antiques and lesser-known paintings. Hot high-end art has no value."

"You know, Lieutenant, I'm trying to get the museum's money back."

"Is that all? What about being the big hero and impressing the museum curator?"

"That's what I'm trying to do, impress. Be the big, rich guy buying questionable art, like you said. You and I are researchers. You research crime and the digestive system. I research the ancients. One thing any researcher knows is that there's no such thing as truth. Facts only exist in religion. Pythagoras never talked about true or false, right or wrong. He talked about limited and limitless. Let me ask you, do you think the universe is limitless?"

"What's that got to do with dipolar Euclidean trigonometry?"

"Limited or limitless?"

"I'll pick limited."

"Here's a Pythagorean dilemma: if you approached the end of the universe, would you be able to stick your arm outside it?"

"I thought Pythagoras was all about the hypotenuse of a triangle."

"Ironically, the Pythagorean theorem is the one thing he didn't discover. To catch the thief, we have to look at patterns like Pythagoreans."

Lowell says, "We each have different angles on the truth. You could have made up all that stuff about finding the pictures by chance. Perhaps you double-crossed another of your cohorts. And now you're far enough away and can't be traced."

"The trouble with that theory, Lieutenant, is that you yourself don't believe it."

Chapter Ten

The Roman Empire was not built by nice guys. Not only did they use force, they celebrated brutality, organized it, paraded it in front of cheering throngs; and when they didn't use it, they threatened to use it. The emperor rode into battle at the head of his army—that's how he got to be emperor in the first place.

Individuals who threatened the emperor's power were tossed naked into coliseums to be mutilated by wild animals or wild men, egged on by cheering crowds. The emperor made it absolutely clear what would happen to rebels and deviants.

Brut force is necessary for a civilization to survive and expand, Paris once wrote in a treatise on the subject. Scholarly rivals criticized the work and attacked Paris as being pro-fascist. Paris is a lot of things, but absolutely not a fascist.

He is a historian, devoted to Athena and Apollo and Orpheus. Odysseus's blood flows through him. A chapter in his best-selling book praises the Alpha Male, the emperor, as vital for the safety and advancement of humanity. The Alpha rules by force and intimidation. Tribes that had no Alpha died out or lived marginally. *Look around,* he wrote. *Nice guy societies don't make it. They need the sword of Athena, and she was anything but a wimp.*

Paris is musing about the time he tried to be an Alpha. "Know thyself," said one philosopher after another. Know thy place in the social order. He's dressed as an elegant millionaire, as Lowell suggested, and reading the *Wall Street Journal,* sitting at the window table of Jordan's, a cafe across from Adler's gallery. He looks up to see what's going on across the road, turns to the paper and scribbles a few notes about stocks he's interested in researching. During the two hours that he's sitting, no one has entered or left the gallery. He makes a few options trades on his phone.

As a waitress brings Paris another pot of jasmine tea, a taxi drops off Dr. Adler. Paris observes intently. He pulls out a picture clipped from a newspaper's society section of Dr. Adler and looks at it while Adler is standing and paying the taxi. The taxi drives off, and Adler walks up the stairs into his gallery. Paris leaves a twenty, like James Bond would do, puts on his coat and scarf, and walks across the street.

The gallery radiates money—even from where Paris is standing outside the door he feels it. He hears classical music from inside. A window poster with a vintage black-and-white photo of a reclining nude announces that the works displayed are of a Czech artist whose pictures hang on the walls and whose sculptures sit on pedestals. Other art is presented, each lit, making them visible through the picture window. Paris sees a nineteenth century lithograph of a scene from late antiquity and studies it. He spots something wrong with it. He knows that the gallery is a front for Adler's real business—dealing with wealthy collectors.

Early in his scholarly career, Paris fantasized being a debonair attired gentleman, one who ate a soft-boiled egg with toast and butter, served on a silver tray with a crocheted hood over the egg cup; who dressed in a turtleneck and sport coat with a silk scarf around his neck; who read Virgil and Tennyson by the fireplace. Yes, Paris had a fantasy of becoming like Dr. Adler. When he watched a James Bond film, he pictured himself in that role—suave, composed, powerful. But wealth and pretense gave him the willies. Instead he became the slogging scholar.

Paris must now own his place in the House of Odysseus. He must be gregarious, debonair and cool, approaching the museum theft from a different angle than Lowell and relying on his friend Barry to dive into the art underworld with him.

He remembers Dr. Adler's name at a conference on ancient art. Adler had a reputation for authenticating antiquities. People who look at this stuff all the time know how each god was painted in different parts of the Mediterranean, what statues are carved where, the different styles of each period and each area. Much of our knowledge about ancient Greece comes from scenes painted on pottery.

Everyone admires Dr. Adler. One look at him and you know he's urbane and intelligent, an unquestioned success. Imogen and Helen react with almost religious respect when his name is mentioned. He's done so much for the museum, especially after the heist. But animal nature tells Paris not to trust this gentleman while rational nature tells him to be careful around a man who has more resources than Paris. He needs to approach Dr. Adler outside his position of power in an arena where they can be equals. Like two wrestlers, the person in the unbalanced position will lose. He must look and act as rich as Adler. If he pays Dr. Adler to procure special pieces necessary for his neo-Pythagorean school, he would take away Adler's advantage; paying for Adler's services would change their hierarchical position.

Wrapped in his coat, his face hidden by a scarf, Paris is standing on the sidewalk looking at Adler's gallery, thinking of what art he needs for his own museum. All the works of Myron of Eleutherae, one of Greece's foremost artists, have been lost, but copies of some were made. He and the others inspired the great legacy of ancient art. It hits him right there that he needs a statue of Orpheus because Pythagoras was inspired by Orpheus; both were musicians who believed that the vibration of strings cured both physical and spiritual disease—*spiritual* to the Greeks meaning *rational.* Why not the famous bust he had in his Apollo Self Storage office called the Tartenum Benedetta Orpheus? It was lost to the world centuries ago. He can make an excellent copy of it.

Paris leaves Newbury Street and returns to his under-construction school, his future Temple of the Muses. He closes his eyes and takes stock of his talents. He's good at creating fake artifacts that fool the world, if only temporarily. He knows the classical world and he knows antiquities. He must use this knowledge to trip Adler. Perhaps instead of fearing

Adler's ability to spot a fake at first glance he can use it con-structively.

He looks around at the basic structure of his museum. He can use the excuse of filling it with antiquities of question-able origin as a way to become enmeshed in the underground, like Orpheus diving into Hades. He has to strategically buy antiquities that wouldn't necessarily belong in a Pythagorean school—he has the money—and sell his forgeries through the right middlemen.

He has to sell his fakes and buy fakes as well as deal in genuine antiquities. His rational mind knows that if he gets caught again, he might get back to that cigar-smoking judge who had a special dislike for the pompous scholar who came from a blue-collar background and was in trouble with the law in his teens.

Four years ago he created an imaginary tribe of seafar-ing nomads trading around the Mediterranean before the time of Homer. He made an amulet from Troy, inscribed it with Homeric Greek, Linear B, and an occasional Phoenician word, and had a team of Swedish archeologists "discover" it in the ancient city of Tharros on the island of Sardinia. Funer-al masks and polychrome vases were "discovered" near the Temple of Selinus in Sicily. A tool showed up that would have pushed back the birth of the Iron Age by a century.

It created a sensation. Paris had more questions than answers for the scholarly community. He presented other astounding facts, a couple of urns with Assyrian pictures and an inscription from ancient Ebla in Syria. *Who were these people?* he asked in a pivotal article in the *Journal of Ancient History.* *Why have we never encountered this tribe before?*

"One of the most potent finds in our lifetime," de-clared an academic from the University of Heidelberg.

Paris rummaged through the vast back corridors of the British Museum and found a numbered Sumerian clay tab-let—which he had actually planted (they check what people take out of special collections, not what they bring in)—which referred to this mysterious but advanced tribe. He started a language to give them from which various Indo-European and Semitic words can be derived.

When the experts ate it up, he closed his office door and basked in his ability to wrap academia around his ridiculous idea and recreate history. In his arrogant magnanimousness, he donated one of his fakes to the university museum, and they treated him like a celebrity, which made him even more pompous.

Like Tantalus, blessed by the gods, who in his arrogance stole from them their sacred ambrosia, Paris tried to steal himself a new position in life. He tried to be an Alpha instead of accepting his destiny. The more he promoted his lie, the more he believed it, like the Piltdown Man hoax where hominoid skull fragments turned up all over England in the early 1900s, a hoax unwittingly assisted by the British Museum.

One scholar from Columbia—whose reputation Paris had trashed years ago—suspected Paris's con. He had one of Paris's fakes in his office and was examining it. It was a vendetta, the stupid fellow and his grudge. Paris had to stop him, get it out of his office.

Paris was hardly able to speak in court. How did a prank get so out of control, destroy his rational mind and take over his life?

If it had been just a matter of Paris breaking into a professor's office, the woman judge who reeked of cigar would have given him a slap on the wrist and told him never to do it again. If it had just been planting false evidence and discovering objects that he had made, a jury would have laughed at his joke. Or if it had been just a matter of passing off fake objects to a museum, the academic community would have been inspired by his cunning.

But the combination of all his crimes, including offering a fake antiquity to his alma mater for fifty K, another attempt to square a grudge, was like telling the judge that she stinks of cigar.

Now, almost four years later, he's going to do it again.

He sits quietly, eyes closed, checking his motivation. He swore an oath to Athena never to be so egocentric again. Although he *told* the judge he wouldn't make another fake, he did not swear an *oath* to her.

He opens his eyes and looks around, picking a space in the eastern corner of the open room where he could set up a work table. He'll need a gas oven and a large toaster oven. He goes out and buys a cheap set of watercolors—the kind given to children—brings in dirt from an empty lot and buys various products from the grocery store, such as tomato juice, tea, milk, and vegetable dye. He needs boric acid, paint thinner, and fiberglass resin hardener from the hardware store. He has already spent years experimenting with these products.

Making forgeries is not high-tech. Those who have passed off successful forgeries used the most rudimentary ingredients. Several forgers have left detailed descriptions of their technique. The important part of the process is giving the item to the right expert in the right way to get his approval. A good forger pulls the viewer's gaze to a certain part of the object and away from seeing the overall. If the viewer first focuses on whether it's real, the battle is lost.

He rents a car on Saturday and goes to antiques dealers in New Hampshire looking for materials he can use. It is easier to age pottery that is already a hundred years old than only a few years old. He buys any unglazed pottery from the nineteenth century he can find, and he finds a lot. He brings them back to his work area, dries them out to make them even lighter, synthesizing two thousand years in forty-eight hours. He paints them with classical myths and then fades the color by grinding in dirt. The artisanship doesn't need to be great; most antiquities don't have great art. When he first started years before, he had to experiment months, trying out dyes and drying techniques. Forgers aim to make their work stand tests for age, though no one could ever make them stand all tests for age. There are scientific ways to date clay, fired and unfired, but few perform these tests. Most pottery of that era was fired at low temperature.

Some of the fakes need to go in Paris's temple, others sold, and one has to be special—Orpheus—that he will give on consignment and be anxious to buy.

***

Paris's first "chance" encounter with Dr. Adler comes at a party for social giving at the Harvard Club on Commonwealth Avenue. Paris—in black tie—is there first, standing near the cut marble fireplace, rich mahogany paneling and ornate mirrors surrounding the room. Other guests are milling about in groups as a piano player's fingers glide over the keyboard producing cozy melodies. It's Christmastime, and everyone is in a joyous mood.

As soon as he sees Adler enter, Paris reminds himself to let Adler come to him, to appear uninterested, to pretend not to be there to meet Adler.

He sees the doorman taking Adler's coat, and Adler dives into the gathering, approaching a group of philanthropists like old friends, pressing the flesh, more like a statesman than a politician. Paris joins a different group and becomes gripped by stimulating conversation about the importance of building another homeless shelter in a part of town he's never heard of. He sees Adler moving to another group, handshaking men and rubbing cheeks with women. He looks like Salvador Dalí.

When Adler approaches Paris's group, Paris remains entranced by his conversation. Adler greets others, then turns to Paris.

"I don't believe I've had the pleasure," Adler says.

Can't trust those eyes, is Paris's first reaction, *ruthless beyond all his chivalry*. But Paris isn't good at people and wonders if it's a superspy caper from his imagination.

"Paris." He says it just like James Bond says, "*Bond*," extending his hand.

Disguise can be necessary to fight for right. Odysseus disguised himself as a beggar when he returned home.

Adler makes an *ah-ha* face as if he didn't know who he was. Paris can see that he is pretending to come to him as casually as Paris is pretending. Scheming businessman.

"Adler. A pleasure."

"Dr. Adler, I'm so happy to meet you. I've been meaning to approach you for your knowledge and ability to acquire art."

The statement comes across as too contrived, but he doesn't think Adler notices since they're both busy sizing each other up.

"The pleasure of sharing art with a gentleman is mine. I understand from my old friend Professor Vecchio that you're building a classical collection here."

"Word spreads fast."

"The classical art world is like a family. Conscientious collectors know each other. I have a feeling we've met."

They hadn't met, but Adler would certainly know of Paris's infamous hoax. "I've been working nonstop in investments." He doesn't say that his work on investments started two months ago. "But I love classical art, and I am turning my attention to building a showplace on a hill dedicated to Pythagoras."

"The first scientist, philosopher, and musicologist."

"The hill being the top floor of an old factory."

"What a brilliant project—a modern palace for learning in the Pythagorean style."

Paris knows that Adler has been told about the project and he's happy that Adler is approaching him like a salesman. As in a wrestling maneuver, Adler has put himself in the lower position. Paris's fear of Adler begins to wane.

"I aim to fill the space with works of art, so it's fortuitous that we meet here by chance."

As he says the words, he's thinking that he had to shell out ten grand to an obscure charity so he could be there for their by-chance meeting.

Adler invites him to the two leather armchairs near them. They remain formal, businesslike, gentlemanly.

"I'll do anything I can to make your dream a reality."

"I insist on original works."

"Imitations are dastardly. Why don't you come to my gallery tomorrow and we'll see how I can help in this noble endeavor."

"I have a good idea of what I need. It's a matter of finding the pieces. I'm right now interested in a frieze of Achilles mourning Patroclus. It comes from the town of Vulci. A collector in Switzerland owns it, and I need an intermediary to help procure it."

"Oh yes, I know objects from there. I'm looking forward to helping you. I'll also look to see what else is available."

"I'll drop by your gallery. I bet you can procure the Mona Lisa." James Bond smile.

"Love and honor one cannot buy, but everything in the material world is available for the right price."

***

Stymied by the news leak, Lowell has to figure out a new tactic. He goes back to the records and pulls out cards for the people who have already been interrogated after the Gardner heist.

Lowell, usually not a desk person, grinds through thousands of pages of notes and interviews conducted over the years. He's specifically not looking for Tizzio—he wants clues that might implicate a sophisticated art lover to the original burglary. The police had dismissed the idea that the burglars were anything but low-level opportunists, which may have limited their investigation. After a week sitting behind his desk, all the while worrying about the amount of cholecystokinin in the stomach, which is essential to breaking down sugars and proteins, Lowell finds one small thread. Six months ago a museum in Rotterdam, Holland, was robbed in broad daylight. The only item stolen was a vase from Syracuse dated from the time of Archimedes. The robbers were caught a few days later and talked to get light sentences, but they didn't know who had hired them. All clues indicate that the item was a special order.

When he meets the commissioner in his posh office,

the commissioner tells him that the likelihood that the robbers have already been interrogated is very high. "The FBI and police rounded up every thief they could find and questioned them. Private reward hunters hounded them even more."

Sitting in a deep armchair across the desk, Lowell says, "Unless the master thief made this his only action. If the burglars were hired by someone they didn't know, we might not have talked to the right person."

"Tizzio for some reason didn't want to turn in the art."

"Maybe he didn't control it. Maybe Tizzio isn't essential to the case."

The commissioner thinks about this. "That might make sense. There's something not right about the whole story. Why wouldn't the thief want to deal? It's been years, and he couldn't do anything else with the art except return it."

"I didn't get the feeling that the thug who used Paris's storage business represented a cultured art figure." Lowell looks at the commissioner, wondering how to bring this up. He says, "What do you make of Paris zeroing in on Adler?"

"You believe his story?"

"It doesn't matter whether or not I believe. I told him to live high, be a sucker. Paris is the only thing we have. He might draw out the thief."

The commissioner nods. He opens a desk drawer and throws a file on the desk in front of Lowell. "You'll want this."

Lowell looks at the title: Ernesto Adler.

The commissioner says, "It's pretty slim because we don't have anything illegal on him. The researcher thinks he has an account in the Cayman Islands, which isn't unusual for a rich business guy. If it's true, his transactions doubtlessly go through that account and remain undeclared."

Lowell says, "If we can cut off his funds, it would make him more eager to make a deal with Paris."

"We're not sure about it. We don't know whose name the account is in, but you'll read in the file why the investigators suspect it belongs to Adler."

Lowell thinks that he must find that bank account and a clever way to squeeze it, hoping that if it is Adler's, he'll come out to do battle. Lowell needs to be active. It's a long shot, but it's the only solid thing he has.

"You'll get zero cooperation from the Cayman Islands," the commissioner says.

"Whoever the thief is, he would be interested in meeting the guy who stole his stash."

"The thief may suspect that one of his own guys betrayed him for the reward, which may be true, especially considering Paris's past. Just make sure to keep Paris's identity secret or we'll be doing a murder investigation. Besides you, only Helen and Imogen know him."

"Another thing we never pondered: the museum was having a hard time when the heist happened. The burglary kick-started a campaign that pulled in millions and got the city to rally around the museum. The place took off after that. Adler and Imogen worked together to bring the museum international fame."

"Imogen is an obstinate character. She'll drive six blocks out of her way and run you over to prove that you were in the wrong."

***

As soon as he leaves the Harvard Club, Paris meets Barry at a Kenmore Square café and tells him about the initial contact. "We have to continue gingerly. We have to buy and sell legitimate as well as questionable art. Are you in?"

"Adler is a smart dude, very respectable. That means you have to be on your toes. Crooks you can count on to be crooks. There's no telling what respectable gentlemen will do. The tricks he pulls might be better than the tricks we pull. But I'm in."

"Adler is tops in his field. We have to contemplate each action, make sure we're not acting from emotion."

"You're going to sell him one of the fakes you're making?"

"No. I'm going to buy it from him."

"In order to get—"

"The Samos vase."

"Hasn't he been looking for it all along?"

"He's been looking for the art that was robbed from the Gardner Museum, that's for sure. He hired detectives and offered a big reward."

"Doesn't that mean that he genuinely didn't know about the robbery?"

Boston University students are coming in and out, spreading cold air in the café every time the door is open. A group of students is talking and laughing around a table. Everyone else is engrossed on a device.

"It means that he genuinely didn't know where the art was," Paris says. "That's all we can conclude." Paris takes a change-the-subject pause. "I have to make a special fake. The museum I'm building is the ideal place to work since I can use the excuse of restoring antiquities for the exhibit."

"Does Lowell know what you're going to do?"

"He wants me out there, living high, attracting attention. Just as long as nobody knows I returned the Gardner art. I think it would be better if you and Lowell didn't meet. He is, after all, a cop, and what we're planning on doing is more than jaywalking. By the way, how's your Italian?"

***

A chime sounds as Paris enters Adler's gallery. He stays alone for a while, hands behind his back, looking at the displayed art. They have absurd prices; Adler probably has to sell only one piece a week to keep the place solvent. Or maybe one a month. Besides, Adler doesn't need the money from his galleries.

The same sales woman he met on the last occasion comes out. He can see that she doesn't remember him. He asks if Dr. Adler is in. She goes to the backroom.

Adler appears, a silk scarf around his neck and a matching handkerchief in his breast pocket and patent-leather Italian shoes on his feet. He has a restrained smile befitting a gentleman. He's not a tall man, moderately slender, moderately dark, groomed mustache.

"I was just passing." As soon as the words come out Paris's mouth he realizes they're trite.

"Mr. Paris, I'm honored to have you grace my gallery. Tell me, is your project part of a partnership?"

"I'm entirely on my own." He must act just as upper class, formally debonair, suave, rich, ready to engage Dr. Adler in a gentleman's competition of out-sophisticating the other.

"You can't possibly undertake such a project by yourself."

"I'm cutting back my hours in investments to devote time to my real love—the classical world. Over the years I've only had time to collect a few rare pieces of antiquity."

He thinks of the forgeries he has to generate to show off his newly-imagined collection. He also sees that Adler is relieved not to have to work with a board or committee.

"Now that it's no longer a secret that I want to re-create an actual Pythagorean school on an urban hilltop, I'm looking for objects, modern and ancient, that would make the place come alive."

"I'll be excited to contribute to this project."

They both speak stiff words.

"I'm looking for certain objects the Pythagoreans used in Southern Italy. I think also things from Pythagoras's hometown of Samos."

"The Island of Samos. Not much exists from there."

"It's not my area of expertise since Samos itself was only a thriving civilization for a few decades, but it produced its greatest native son."

"I'll do everything I can to help an active collector."

"I prefer to think of myself more as a person of taste than as a collector."

"That's why you came into my studio. A gentleman of the old school. Not many of us left. Professor Vecchio already told me that you specialize in *Magna Graecia*."

"I wouldn't call it a *specialty* but an *outlook*, a way of perceiving the world." Paris keeps a snooty tone, a detached expression.

"Then we agree on original works?"

"Everything is copied from the Greeks, our art and sculpture, our buildings and cities, our science and letters."

"Exactly my sentiments."

"I know you too are an expert in the golden age of art," Paris says.

"The fifth and fourth centuries BC stimulate me most."

"Pythagoras and his school were the avant-garde of that era. I'm already negotiating to buy a lyre that survives. It's from a museum in—oh I shouldn't mention it since negotiations are still pending. Pythagoras inspired those in his community by playing his lyre in the middle of his school, just like Orpheus."

This is Paris's introduction of Orpheus. He looks to see if Adler reacts, but sees nothing. That's good. He'll soon hear more about Orpheus.

"It's always better to work through an agent. We have a sense of the market and negotiate the best prices."

"That is, indeed, why I walked into your gallery. Price is secondary. But everything must be authentic."

"I never use the word *replica*."

"I'd also like objects of a later period that depict the classical world, but they must be absolutely historically correct."

Paris looks at the nineteenth century lithograph he saw last time when he peeked in the window. It shows a scene of a Christian maiden deciding whether to make a pagan sacrifice or be thrown to the lions. Behind her is Rome's Coliseum.

"Look at this. We can see that this takes place in Rome during the Diocletian persecution. But his edicts had no impact in Rome where Augustus Chlorus reigned. This martyr belongs in Antioch or Alexandria or during a previous persecution."

"A wise observation."

"It's wrong and thus valueless. Shall I destroy it right now?"

Paris takes a step forward to grab the frame. He's dead serious. Odysseus ready to pounce on immorality.

Adler stumbles, puts his hand on Paris's shoulder as Paris is grabbing the sides of the frame, ready to rip it off the wall and trample it. Adler is apologetic, and Paris realizes that he has gained the position of power.

"Well, actually, it's on consignment. I must return it. I never wanted it here, but you know there are so many pressures."

Paris reluctantly backs off. Cunning Odysseus has demonstrated his principles and sophistication. He says, "I have, for example, a tablet from Minoan Crete of monsters serving as satyrs. It shows clearly both cults of Apollo and Dionysus the way the Pythagorean school portrayed them, demonstrating Pythagoras's influence around the Mediterranean. It's worn, of course, but some details are clear, showing an artist who lived the era."

Paris thinks this up on the spot; now he has to make it and make it badly to show that, although he knows history, he doesn't know the difference between genuine and fake objects.

Adler tries to recoup his poise. "It would give me great joy to see this treasure."

"It's an honor to share art with a gentleman. As Samos was the birthplace of Pythagoras, Crete is Zeus's home and his first wife Wisdom."

Paris hands Adler his calling card, saying, "I have it on good authority that you're a trusted dealer who can procure the most obscure piece."

Dr. Adler looks at the card. Paris can see Adler thinking about making money off Paris.

"An interesting address, right in an industrial area. I was thinking of the area myself since its being transformed into an arts district. Shall we say tomorrow at the same time?"

Paris needs much more time to prepare his fakes, but

he likes that Adler is anxious to do business as soon as possible.

"I'm off to a conference," Paris says. "I still have employees in my venture capital firm. How about next week at the same time?"

They agree. Adler shows him out the door with affected civility.

Chapter Eleven

An art dealer and Paris sit next to each other on straight-back chairs in the middle of the bare Pythagorean triangle in the center of the temple, a folder and notebook on an improvised table in front of them. It's still a construction zone. The art dealer is showing photos of antiquities. He wears his plaid suit like a bygone salesman who knocked on doors selling encyclopedias. Paris examines one of the photos.

"This is difficult to get," the dealer says. "It's outside the country and illegal to import."

"I certainly wouldn't ask you to do anything illegal."

The dealer crosses and uncrosses his legs. "We don't do anything illegal. We abide by the law to the letter."

"I wouldn't dream of asking you to do the most minimal action outside the law."

"There are people who can procure these objects, but not us."

"And how much do you think these people would want for their trouble?" Paris doesn't mask his sarcasm. He knows that the illegal-to-import idea is a ruse. They want to keep it secret because, Paris can see from the photo, the object is obviously a forgery.

"I have to repeat that we don't have anything to do with such things. People who deal with special orders would probably want two hundred fifty thousand."

"Why, that's robbery—robbery twice over. I wouldn't pay more than half that."

"Of course, I don't know much about their business, but I would guess that it's far too little. Perhaps they would settle for two hundred."

Paris waves his hand dismissively. "My price is adequate. If these people don't want to sell, we'll just let it go."

"I'm sure you can find a number in between."

"If it's more than one twenty-five, you can keep it."

"Of course, you'll have to settle with them."

"And when do you think these people can have it for me?"

"They work fast."

"Before the buyer has the chance to change his mind." He doesn't care if he sounds caustic.

"I'm sure you can have it within forty-eight hours."

"Cash?"

"I believe that's their way. They usually have a warehouse where transactions are made. I don't have anything to do with it."

"Of course."

Paris has a glimpse of the absurdity, spending a hundred and twenty-five thousand on something he knows is a fake. He can create a better one himself. And having to deal with a slug. But he has to get the word out that he's a soft touch who can't tell a fake from a real antiquity. He never knows when he'll stumble on the right underground figure who has the Samos vase. Although he's aiming for Adler, he has to stay open to the entire art underworld and presumably word will get around.

"I might have something these people may be interested in," Paris says.

He moves to another area and picks up a wooden box, handing it to the dealer. It's an authentic marble head of Septimius Severus that he bought two days ago from another slimebag. Septimius's wife went overboard praising Pythagoras's divine origin from Apollo to rival the divine origin of Jesus whose cult was expanding exponentially.

"Please have someone look this over and tell me if they're interested." Paris knew when he bought it that he would lose on the deal.

The doorbell rings. Paris stands, and so does the art dealer. They don't shake hands. Paris accompanies him to the door. When he opens it, Helen enters with a canvas bag. She gives the art dealer a cold stare, but they exchange only glances. Paris sees that she recognizes him. He isn't surprised but would rather that she not know what he's up to, which is probably impossible.

"Let me know," Paris says to him.

The dealer exits without a word, and Paris closes the door.

"What kind of people are you dealing with?" She's more shocked than chastising.

"He's just a middleman."

"Look, Paris. Since our theft we've been in contact with sleazy guys like him, thinking one of them would lead to the paintings. They wear suits, and some have art degrees, but they're like drug dealers or bank robbers. What are you doing with them?"

They walk together into the marble room. "I'm not buying anything from him."

"Let me guess—you're buying from a mysterious third party? You put up cash, and the object appears in your living room. Many items are fraudulent. They can't work on the open market."

He waves both hands around the room. "I need to make this the perfect neo-Pythagorean school. I studied exactly how it should be."

"Dealing with those types will destroy your reputation before you've had time to build it."

Paris thinks that he is, indeed, trying to ruin his reputation. It's a sacrifice to the gods.

"Someone picks up the object from a warehouse."

"They like to work out of the airport cargo terminals where people pick up and drop off shipments. They're paranoid about being tracked down, so they deal through salesmen like him."

They're near the center of the enormous, mostly empty, room. He goes to a dusty side table, opens it and brings out a bottle of wine and his two glasses. She looks at the label, a 1982 Tuscan Sassicaia.

"Private reserve," Paris says. He feels mischievous

bringing it out. He didn't buy it for her to pretend that he's part of her sophisticated world. He just wanted to do something nice for her. "It was a real bargain—under two hundred a bottle when you buy a case."

Despite the sadness of losing the thief because of the news leak, they're both in a jolly mood. She sips. Paris sees that she immediately recognizes the fullness of the wine. He realizes that since they met, he's been so obsessed in building that he's hardly had a chance to see her, and now he's engrossed in a different endeavor which may alienate her.

She puts down her glass and hands her canvas bag to Paris. He takes out the wrapping and sees the copy of the missing Samos vase. He suddenly turns quiet and serious, examining carefully, touching and studying its worn image. It features a rough scene of Iphigenia and Clytemnestra. He turns it in his hand and looks at it like a jeweler examining a rough diamond.

"A surprisingly good copy," he says.

"It was made while Isabella was still alive. I'm not sure why."

"Maybe someone was trying to prove something. I'll put it in the temple section of the school. Promise me that you won't tell anyone that you're loaning it to me."

"Why?"

"Just promise. Don't even tell Imogen. The real one is our link with the thief."

He doesn't tell her that he's already working on getting the three other vases that were part of the set.

"I promise, but if the police can't find the thief, what makes you think you can?"

He says, "I believe Euripides's version that Artemis carried Iphigenia to the Tauridans at the top of the Black Sea where she became priestess. Sacrifice is a major tenant of myth. We have to fast or do penance in order to receive a reward. Every society glorified the ultimate sacrifice of warriors. But they didn't have ritual human sacrifice at the time of the Trojan War. The Biblical story of God staying Abraham's hand signifies the end of human sacrifice."

They look at each other. Paris again is grinning; he should stop lecturing, but how far should he make an advance toward her? "One day I'll catch you doing something uncool."

"I have this feeling that you think I'm a joke," Helen says.

"Maybe we take ourselves too seriously."

She looks around the room. "You know all about this—classics that is."

"My ex says that I still live in that era."

"How did it start, your love of the ancients?"

"There was this teacher in high school. She was dark, mysterious and beautiful. I would do anything to get her attention. She told us she was going to teach us about myth. It wasn't the type of school that taught the finer facets of life, if you know what I mean, and the course wasn't about mythology. It was social studies, but a couple of classes were going to be about Greek myths. I went home and read a lot about them for a week to impress her. I stayed up all night reading, so when the first class came, I was wiped out and made a fool of myself."

"But you kept studying."

"The stories captivated me." He stands in front of her. Both have wine glasses in their hands. "I felt an emptiness in this world. In ancient times they had community. They touched life, lived as if it could be their last day, which it could well have been. They lived with danger and fear, had to work for their bread. We solved many of these problems. We don't die of famine. Our lifespan is more than twice as long as theirs. We have insulated coats and microwave ovens, heated homes and flush toilets, cars and jets. I got to wondering if we would be able to take the good in their world and put it in ours."

"You think they lived better than we do?"

"Socially. People gathered in the agora and the streets. Now we're alone in our cars, and we run over children if they're in the street. We're isolated, locked inside our homes.

Our friends are television personalities. We're inactive, obese. We made physical advances over the centuries. We have healthy bodies, all our teeth, and know a thousand times as much as they knew. But we don't know more today about who we are than they did, only now our agony is greater because we see farther with our telescopes and smaller with our microscopes. We have library after library of experiments and measurements. We have pictures from space, robots scanning the bottom of the ocean."

"It's funny you say all that given that you're not the most social creature to walk the earth."

Just then he realizes that his rants are anti-social since they turn into a one-sided conversation. He lowers his head and steps back.

"Why don't we stay in the present, at least for the next half hour," she says.

A tactful way of telling him to shut up. He perks up and switches gears. "I made a stunning discovery. I spotted you in a Charles Street restaurant and observed your weakness for decadent desserts."

He saw her with a gentleman, wasn't jealous, figured it was part of her calling.

"Don't tell Imogen. We both swore that we'd each lose two pounds this month."

"This Pythagorean school threatens to become a den of diabolical secrets."

Helen is kind, he thinks, and although she seems formal, he sees a wicked sense of fun underneath. He wonders if she has the same conflicted thoughts about the relationship as he has.

"And I discovered something about you," she offers.

"Don't tell me that you unmasked my addiction to mystery novels."

"Worse. I discovered that you almost bought a seventeenth century frieze made in a Catholic monastery."

"My pagan friends would be scandalized."

"And I learned that you rarely cook vegetables."

"You found out from Lowell. He picks up details about people, especially what they eat, and he's been following me too closely. He wants to know my bathroom habits. Right now I'm his only suspect. But we should never forget that the thief has the real Samos vase, not this copy here. If we find the vase, the thief comes with it."

***

Later that week, Barry gets off a rickety warehouse freight elevator carrying a briefcase. He's greeted by a fence dressed as a warehouse clerk. Barry observes the man's downturned mouth which seems etched on his face—a face unable to smile or present anything other than anguish, with craters on his cheeks as if life struck him with meteorites of grief and disappointment. Barry glances around. The place looks seedy enough without the fence, but his presence gives Barry the feeling of wanting to run out and shower, and Barry is no Mr. Clean.

"I'm delivering prints and collecting enlargements," Barry says, trying to get a bead on the fellow.

The guy reminds him of losers he met when he was inside, guys who had given up on everything except disappointment. The fence gives a cocky head-shake; his open, white shirt shows strands of gold chains supporting a saint medal, and there's a fat, bright-red stone on his pinkie.

"Have I come at the right time?" Barry asks.

The fence acknowledges with the most minimal throat noise, takes him to a counter and hands him a plywood box. He pulls out a screw gun and shoves it across the counter at Barry without raising his head. Barry unscrews the top screws, takes out the packaging and then lifts a Greek-era bust out of the box. He glances at it, then puts it back, opens his briefcase and hands the fence a bundle wrapped in paper.

"I don't count. I like to start off a relationship with trust."

A strange statement from someone who oozes distrust.

"Who shall I say the delivery is from?" Barry asks.

"I don't know names. I'm the shipping agent, like you."

Barry walks back to the elevator. "I think we have something from our end coming in a couple of days."

The fellow doesn't acknowledge, either in voice or gesture, just goes back to a ledger and writes something as if Barry is an apparition.

***

Paris makes little effort to clear up the area where he makes fakes before Dr. Adler's visit. His corner for forging antiquities looks like a place to clean objects and polish stones that will be installed in the museum. There isn't much there that would give away what he's doing: paints, an oven and solutions in jars, matching the entire floor which looks like a construction site.

Nor is he dressed like a gentleman, but he does put on a cunning Odysseus grin as Adler enters. Adler is dressed debonair as always, and just then Paris's throat constricts. Is his scheme nonsense? Perhaps it's out of jealousy that he's after Adler. Adler is unquestionably a decent and learned man. He loves art and loves the museum. How can Paris possibly suspect this man?

What Paris is planning might bring his whole world down, destroy the gift the gods have given him. What's he got on Adler? Absolutely nothing. Not one thing. Who does he think he is, a fancy international spy?

He should entertain Adler, then bow out and let Lowell do his job. He must concentrate on his life's dream of presenting Pythagoras to the world—he's so close to that dream—the gods have made it possible. What can be a clearer divine gift than stumbling on ten million dollars? Instead, he's illogically fixated on Dr. Adler, and that obsession could not only erase his money but also throw him back in prison. *Get your priorities straight*, he says to himself as he takes Adler's coat.

But there's something funny about that Samos vase and he can't stop thinking that Adler is connected to it.

Adler looks around the room. Paris distracts him with

business. "By the way, were you able to find out about that frieze of Achilles mourning Patroclus?"

"I discovered that it would be difficult to import. There are so many rules that govern exporting antiquities, but it can be done with the right pedigree papers."

"And how much do those papers cost?"

"Depends on which channels we have to go through. New York has gotten too complicated, but Miami is much more amenable."

Now this reputable gentleman shows his colors. They walk around the room.

"I knew to trust you. While other dealers are trapped on highways, you find the untraveled byways."

"I think we can get it to you for about eight hundred, all included."

"I expected to pay over a million. Let's do it. I can write you a check right away."

This is a lie. He figured it is worth half that.

"Only pay on delivery. I learned that the hard way."

"You're so honest, Dr. Adler. The Pythagoreans praised honesty. That's a quality they saw in Orpheus, who they adored. One of my first thoughts for the school was to have original Orpheus-cult material from Magna Graecia."

He wonders whether he's too obvious pushing the Orpheus, and he hasn't even started making it.

"That's much rarer, I'm sure you know, but I'll keep my antennae raised. I may have something else of interest."

"It must be original," Paris says.

"Some people hang reproductions of Monet water lilies on their wall to show they're sophisticated. Even if it's the greatest reproduction, it's not from the artist's own hands and has no feeling."

"But we too are frauds. We did not paint the Monet or chisel the Michelangelo. A real artist would only put his own creations on the wall. A real artist would decorate his own house with his own art.

"You may be going to extremes. A complete artist

would have to build his own house using raw materials—chopping trees and gathering stone. He would make his own furniture, weave his own rugs, glaze his own mirrors from sand, polish his own stones for jewelry. A real artist would shear wool from sheep and pick cotton, spin it and weave his own clothes like they did before we had cities, spending every hour of the day making things."

Very good. He's engrossing Adler in a gentleman's philosophical argument where he can be on a higher footing.

"Let me show you what I intend to do with this space."

Paris walks Adler around the area, describing how it will be, pointing and gesturing. He casually leads Adler to two items that he made. Adler looks at the first piece with a frown.

"Oh this. Do you like it?" Paris's voice is proud. "This is a scene from Palmyra. Pythagoras passed through there on his way to Mesopotamia."

"Where did you get it?"

Adler's bewildered voice shows that he spotted it as a fake. It isn't even a good fake. He made it deliberately badly.

"A dealer from New York offered it to me exclusively."

He enthusiastically shows another obviously fake antiquity and sees Adler's perplexed face. It's another low-category fake to prove to Adler that he's a chump.

"And it was authenticated?" Adler asks.

"Oh yes. I have a certificate, but the owner didn't want people to know it was being sold. It's from Carthage. I suspect Pythagoras visited the city when he was about thirty. Isn't it lovely?"

Adler forces a smile. Paris can practically see Adler thinking about making easy money off his new client. For all his sophistication, when it comes to money, Dr. Adler is as ruthless as any successful businessman, and that's good.

***

An art auction is in progress for a small audience in a Westin hotel room near Copley Place. Paris enters and sees Helen in the back row. He walks over and sits on the empty chair next to her.

"Have I missed anything?"

"Not unless you took a sudden interest in Polynesian carvings of chubby women."

"There was a minor detail that I had to attend to. I invested in a small company just before they announced a government contract, and I wanted to see if the stock would go up the eleven percent I predicted."

"And did it?"

"Eighteen percent. People don't know how to value shares. I only invested half a million, although some of it was leveraged in options."

"Then you'll be able to take me to a nice dinner."

"I hired a chef and waiter to cook for the two of us in a private residence on Friday to celebrate the deal. I need to go to New York tomorrow to buy a special item for my museum."

"I'll be coming empty-handed."

"Wherever you go you bring joy and happiness."

They turn away from each other, both avoiding the intensity of the remark, looking up at the next piece being auctioned. A man in a suit brings a painting forward and puts it on an easel in front of the auctioneer's podium.

Paris says, "I'm waiting for a special urn from Rhodes that was in the collection of an estate with the dubious name Belgrade Hollinger."

"It means that the pedigree is unknown. You should stay away from that type of object."

"I looked at it. It's authentic."

"You know just by looking?"

"When you know this stuff, all you have to do is touch it."

The auctioneer announces the seventeenth-century painting for bid, gives a two-sentence description that Paris doesn't hear. Within seconds, the bidding goes up and up in a frenzy.

When the highest bidder wins, Helen says, "Much more than the piece is worth."

"That's what makes auctions interesting. People lose their reason and allow their animal nature—seeing other people bidding and out-bidding makes you want it more."

They sit as various other pieces are auctioned. When the Rhodes urn comes up, Paris whispers to Helen that it is the one he wants.

The auctioneer announces the piece and starts at fifty thousand. No one bids for a long time. He lowers to forty. One hand rises. Forty-five, another hand, and so on until he gets to one twenty. Paris raises his hand, and the bidding continues until one hundred and fifty-five—Paris being the highest bidder.

"Why would this be part of your Pythagorean school? And why would you want it if you don't know where it came from?"

"I'm sure I can sell this for twice the amount that I paid"

"Are you now dealing in art?"

"You have to collect a bunch of items and keep the nice stuff. It's like panning dirt from the bottom of a stream, sifting it, throwing out the dredge and keeping the gold."

"But it's questionable art. Don't you care about that?"

Paris notices her perplexed face, the first time she reveals a negative emotion, and he feels bad keeping her in the dark about what he's doing, but Odysseus had to keep his return to Ithaca secret even from his faithful wife.

***

Lieutenant Lowell follows Barry's taxi from outside Paris's studio to a high-rise on Jamaica Pond. Lowell stops half a block behind the taxi and watches Barry walk into the building. Barry is dressed in his normal untidy look and has a backpack. Lowell notices him handling it more carefully than people handle backpacks. After a minute, Lowell too walks to the door and types redial on the intercom, which tells him the apartment number. While Barry is inside, Lowell phones the commissioner for information about the apartment's owner, all the while thinking that it's strange to ask the commissioner to look up trivial information, what he would normally ask a junior person to check.

But the commissioner is in a jovial mood and hunts for the information on a police website, telling Lowell what they both thought to be true—the apartment is owned by someone who was once investigated but never convicted of art fraud. The commissioner reads to Lowell how he was accused by a London gallery of selling them a fake, but the gallery couldn't prove that he had sold it to them knowingly. The district attorney tried to stick him with other fraudulent art sales, but couldn't get a single indictment.

"Paris found those guys pretty quick," the commissioner says, his voice expressing admiration, a quality Lowell rarely hears in the commissioner's voice.

"That's what he and his friend do: sit and research."

"You think his suspicion of that trustee Adler has merit?"

"If it doesn't, it might bring out the person who has the vase."

A few minutes later, Lowell sees an empty taxi pull up. Barry walks out the main door, this time without a backpack but with a package in a paper grocery bag. He follows Barry back to Paris's future museum. This isn't the first time he's followed Barry and seen such dealing.

***

Paris makes the most of his short trip to New York, stopping first at the Metropolitan Museum, one of his favorite haunts. As a novice academic, he had spent weeks examining their extensive Greek-Roman collections. Museums keep the majority of their acquisitions in back rooms accessible only to scholars.

He plans his trip for when the Metropolitan Opera is staging a Greek tragedy, this time it's Strauss's *Ariandne auf Naxos*, which he will attend in the evening.

But Paris has two other pieces of business, first to sell

and then to buy, and in both cases they are legitimate artifacts. The sell is a two-piece set of terracotta oil lamps from Carthage, which, despite their beauty and impressive detail, don't belong in his collection. He's hoping not to lose too much on the exchange. He bought them to become someone's customer and expand his profile.

His primary mission in New York is to buy the first of the three Samos vases. It had taken a lot of work to track them down, but he feels confident that he's located all three and now has to negotiate to buy them. A New York dealer had arranged the sale of the first from a French private collection. The dealer is warning him that although the one he's buying today will cost only twenty thousand dollars, the second and third will be expensive because they will know that someone wants them.

In jest Paris asks, "And the fourth vase?"

"Victim of the Gardner heist. Few collectors know about it because it's not famous like the other stolen items."

"If you were me, how would you try to get the fourth vase?"

"I wouldn't try. It's a dangerous piece to own, and there's no reward in it—the reward was already given."

Of course, Paris thinks. He has to find a way to offer a lot of money to lure it out of hiding.

When the dealer puts the vase in Paris's hand, Paris feels a thud in his stomach which tells him it's real. It has that look and feel of Samos. Artisans there painted in a particular constrained style. He examines it at arm's length, taking in the entire object and then leaning in for a detailed look. Not an object of great beauty, ordinary for its time, but very few objects of that fifty-year period in Samos' history survive. It doesn't have anything to do with Pythagoras, but he'll pretend.

He will wait until he gets all three before he displays them in his studio, and he's prepared to pay whatever inflated price is quoted.

Chapter Twelve

Next week Paris and Lieutenant Lowell meet at the small park around the Bunker Hill obelisk, the city skyline in the background. A few tourists are taking pictures. Everyone is wearing a thick coat. Paris is carrying a plain wooden box. The two find a bench and sit. Paris gives the box to Lowell who opens it and takes out a bust, examining it minutely. He puts his ear to it and taps it, rubs his fingers all over it, studies it again.

"Am I both supposed to know about this and not know about it?" Lowell asks.

"How old do you think it is?"

Lowell hunches his shoulders.

"Guess," Paris encourages.

"Two thousand years?"

"Three weeks."

"You made it? Why are you telling me?"

"I'm the bait, remember? I can't just lie around like a limp worm on a hook. I've got to be more like a lure, speeding through the water, glittering and attracting attention."

"And why do you reckon the fish will be drawn to it?"

"A certain lover of the arts will be drawn to the bait not for a love of art but because it's sparkling with easy money and, at the same time, the desire to unload an indicting object—the stolen Samos vase."

"When you did this before, you never heard of Tizzio?"

"What I did in the past was a practical joke that went out of control. Everybody knows that. I wasn't in it for money, and I never bought or sold art." Paris stops to correct himself. "Only once, to settle a score." He wants to be as open with Lowell as Lowell seems to be with him. "I never heard of Tizzio, and I don't care about Tizzio. I'm not doing this to make myself richer."

"If you get yourself caught at this, well, you know what will happen."

"I imagine it wouldn't be good for your reputation either."

"The commissioner would ask me serious questions. The press would jump on him in no time. It's a hot topic. He won't be able to defend you."

"One thing I don't understand: if Tizzio makes money in other ways, why would he need to rob a museum?"

"The biggest museum theft ever. Some people who worked on the case had the sense that Tizzio didn't have the pictures but was looking all over for them. I imagine after all these years, he's not happy that someone else found them. Anyway, lots of cops have worked this case to death and haven't turned up anything. What makes you think you can?"

"Helen asked me the same question. I do business; the cops don't. And they don't know antiquities. I don't think it was a coincidence that the Samos vase wasn't in the storage unit."

"A word of advice: don't give a lot of bull if you ain't got much cattle."

"I already learned that." He pauses, looks at Lowell. "You don't care about Tizzio either, do you?"

"It's hard to care about someone who's as hard to grab as the morning dew. I'm not sure why you care about Adler but I'll go along with it because he's so well connected."

"I've been trying to balance animal and rational nature. When I close my eyes and imagine the Samos vase, Adler is sitting right next to it. They're related."

"One thing I doubt that you and Barry found out about Adler: he might have a bank account in the Cayman Islands. The commissioner isn't sure, and he doesn't think it's in his name, but I have a number. People like him put their money into accounts that can't be traced. Switzerland and the Cayman Islands are countries that support terrorism, human trafficking, the mafia, and rich tax-evaders. If we close down their banks, we'd eliminate half the world's crime."

"Why do you suspect the account belongs to Adler?"

"Acetylcholine."

"What's that?"

"A chemical that squeezes the muscle layers in the intestinal tract. When I felt it, it told me that that account matters. But even if the account belongs to Adler, the best we can do is put a temporary hold on it."

"You mean, even if it's impossible to find who owns it, you can strangle it?"

"Temporarily, according to the commissioner."

Paris thinks about this for a long while. They watch a group of bundled up tourists walk quickly down the street.

"That's exactly what we need, a man desperate to make a trade, a fellow acting from animal nature. His leverage would erode. People do crazy things for money. We must exploit him at a vulnerable moment. I'll get the bait right in front of him."

***

That evening Paris takes Helen to a swanky private restaurant in the South End. They are escorted to a special room in the back where they dine alone. Two waiters, dressed better than both of them, are at their service. The chef enters and describes the meal he is about to prepare. The sommelier shows them four bottles, Helen chooses one, and he opens and lets it breathe.

Paris is proud of himself for being able to impress. He knows that Helen's class is style, not money.

"Boston has more possibilities than where I was," Paris says.

Helen starts to talk, checks herself, and then begins again. "It's awkward having a relationship with someone when I'm not supposed to ask anything about him. I feel that I'm stepping on a grenade if I ask a personal question."

"Honestly, I'm embarrassed by my past. The gods have been good to me, giving me gift after gift. They got me out of what was sure to be a life as a delinquent. They got me to study in Cambridge with the best scholars alive. They of-

fered me field work and led me to places where I made finds
that thousands of others missed. They made me one of the
youngest associate professors at a prestigious university. They
brought me stature, something my soul was craving, but I
turned around and double-crossed them. And I didn't want
you to know what idiotic things I did. Starting here from
scratch is a liberation, a rebirth."

"Does Lowell know you?"

"Everything. Another cop would have arrested me for
the Gardner theft, but his curmuring tells him to look out for
me."

"Curmuring?"

"What he calls the low rumbling sound of the bowels."

Paris thinks about telling her more details of his past,
his disgrace, his scorn of gods and men, his relationship with
Alice. He wants to level with her, tell her what he did, but it
would be too great a coincidence when she finds out that he's
at it again—dealing in forged classical art--and she's sure to
find out.

Almost as if he's voicing this, she asks, "Were you a
criminal?"

It's like Sisyphus dropping his boulder on his head.

"Did anyone tell you?"

They're sitting forward close to each other. She shakes
her head. "Just by how you talked about yourself."

"Yes, I was a criminal. In my youth and some years
ago."

"You went to jail?"

"Prison. I served two years."

"For what?"

He can't go further with this. Not at this time. He can't
tell her that it's about forged art: it would be like Orpheus
looking back at Eurydice, but he also can't lie to her.

"For what?" she asks again. There's kindness in her
voice. She wants to understand.

"Well, I can't tell you right now."

"You can't or you won't."

"I will. I want to tell you everything, but not now. Please don't tell Imogen. She already distrusts me."

"Isn't prison supposed to make people worse?"

Paris remains intent on her. "Sit for two years inside a cell and you'll either lash out at the world or make sure you never let anything like that get out of control again. When you hit rock bottom, you can either dig or climb."

They pause, sit back to clear the heavy air. The waiter comes just in time to deliver the appetizer. She says, "Ok, You ask me something personal now."

"Are you as well put-together as you seem?"

Right away he's shocked by what came out of his mouth. He doesn't have much confidence in personal encounters, and the statement reinforces his timidity, but she seems to like the question.

"I suppose I aim to look like that. It's how I am—organized, but I have a dissatisfaction. I wanted to be an artist. I was determined, despite not-gentle advice, until I read *Death of a Salesman* in college. That play is so full of deeper meaning that professors explore, but the one thing I caught was that the salesman was in the wrong profession. He was great with his hands and should have built things, but instead he became a salesman and he was a disaster. I took it personally. Rather than continue beating my head into the right shape and become an artist, I aimed to do what I'm good at, which is curator."

"You're satisfied with your life?"

Helen puts down her fork and knife. Paris sees her thinking as if she had never before thought about that question. "What does satisfaction mean? That I like my job?"

"Americans always think of their job first, but personal satisfaction is more than job."

"That's what I told Lowell when I showed him around the museum. I don't know how anyone can rate satisfaction. I would have been a frustrated artist, but now I see art when I walk down the street and look at buildings, when I'm inside an airport terminal. Our streets are the art we create. This room is art, the way we dress and talk."

Paris, sitting on the edge of his chair, begins his preaching slowly. "I often wonder what future societies would find exciting about us. We look at the ancient world and are fascinated by urns and piles of stones that once formed a room. Perhaps a couple of thousand years from now they'll be excavating our airport terminals, refineries, aircraft carriers. Maybe they'll be able to determine our thoughts and impulses."

He looks to see if she's still paying attention, then continues. "We all put on façades, and then a strange thing happens: we become the person we imitate. The waitress puts on her suit and becomes a waitress. Nurse's uniforms make them care for people. The prisoner takes his role. We don't create, we follow. That's what's exciting about history—every so often someone makes something new. If we all follow what others have done, it may be good and useful, but a real innovator brings us to a new level. You can say the same about science."

"This has turned into a very intellectual discussion."

He stops, apologizes. James Bond has turned into a nerd.

"I had an agreement with my ex that when I started on a rant, she would tell me to stop."

"I don't want to control you. If you want to rant, go ahead. When I get tired of it, I'll let you know. But I do want to know who you are. And I want to know why you won't tell me."

Paris thinks about this. He's too much in rational nature. Romance is animal. He understands that they can't go any further without his explanation. He starts to say, stops himself. It may spoil Lowell's trap. Odysseus honors his word.

***

When Barry enters Paris's place after one of his clandestine drops, Paris is hunched over an illuminated work table magnifier with a pair of tweezers, inserting specks of dust into cracks in the Orpheus statue. In countries that have ancient sites like Luxor or Carthage, entrepreneurs create assembly-line factories for making fakes and passing them off to gullible tourists. Anyone with minimum experience can tell they're fake, but Paris has to be much better, making a fake that will be tested for authenticity by an expert. Every square inch has to be treated—*oldized*, Paris calls it.

"This is the special one," Paris says. "It has to be the best; only the finest authentication expert would see that it isn't real."

"And you're counting on this expert to spot it as a fake."

"Exactly."

Barry looks around. "What am I supposed to call this place? An ancient temple? A Pythagorean school? A museum?"

"All three. I don't know what to call it myself."

He shows Barry the Orpheus statue. "If you were Lowell, would you suspect that I was part of the burglary?"

"No brainer, given your past."

"But he's helping us."

"As long as you're as attractive as honey to a swarm of bees."

Paris puts down the statue. "How did the latest exchange go?"

Barry hands him the box. He opens it and takes out the antique ceramic bust inside. Paris examines it intimately, stroking it, looking closely at the cracks, the dirt in the cracks, the dye used to paint it. He rubs a little water on part of it, checks the density of the clay.

"One of the best fakes I've seen. I didn't doubt it would be good. I think it was made by a Turk. They oldized it well to get our business."

He gives it back to Barry. They remain sitting around Paris's work table.

"A fellow of the trade knows what to look for," Barry says. "You can make one like it yourself."

"We need to do business with these people. We're becoming known in their circle. We don't know which channels Adler works, but we have to get close to him. We need him to know that I buy questionable antiquities. The Samos vase follows."

"I never knew art was such a big business," Barry says. "Never imagined so many crooks."

"Most forged art is never detected. It hangs on museum walls or in private collections, never questioned. People think that it takes extraordinary talent to create a fake. Forgers use simple methods, like soaking the product in Lipton tea, drying it in a toaster oven, rubbing backyard dirt into it. Start with old material and paints that might have been used in that era, then doctor them up, harden them, age them. The main thing is to know the era, how they dressed, what shades of colors and shapes they used. There are countless examples of fakes fooling experts, of museums spending millions acquiring what turn out to be really bad imitations. One Dutchman created fake Vermeers and sold them to the highest ranks of the Nazis after art connoisseurs and experts determined that they were authentic. When he was charged with cooperating with the Nazis, he confessed that they were fakes he had created. No one believed him. The fakes he made were considered Vermeer masterpieces by the tops in the field. They were featured in museums. He had to paint another phony Vermeer in jail to prove himself, but the most interesting part is that the paintings, once praised as the greatest work Vermeer produced, were incredibly bad art. It sheds new light on art experts."

"Forgery is a subject you know well," Barry says.

"eBay is full of people selling antiquities. How many of them do you think are original? They give slips that guarantee originality, but the slips are as easy to make as the fake objects they guarantee. People don't look for the right thing when they look at an object. The secret is to distract them by pulling their attention away from the whole object and to a glaring part of it. Ask any magician. They draw attention to something specific so the audience won't be able to see what's obvious."

"Aren't you afraid of getting caught again?"

"I swore an oath to Helen. Back in the old days, a person's word counted. Today honor is meaningless. Leaders give their word then renege. An oath has become quaint." He looks at the statue he's making. "We're aiming for one vital transaction."

Barry points to the item he brought. "The guy who gave me this says he doesn't know anyone. You got something for me to give him in return?"

"Several. We're buying and we're selling. Soon we'll make it known to everyone that we want the Samos vase."

He takes an oil lamp out of the oven using tongs.

"An expert would recognize this from the Sanctuary of Asclepius in Pergamon, made during the Third Macedonian War."

"Did you copy it from an existing item?"

"I got it from my head, but it's got everything right. You can't tell it's a fake by the images on it. You need to do advanced tests on the material used, which they won't do because we'll put it in the hands of an expert and have him talk about its historical value rather than whether it's a fake."

The two look at the object, which Paris is holding with tongs. He says, "I have to oldize it more before doctoring it up."

"Is an art dealer going to handle the sale?"

"If it's a fake, dealers won't have anything to do with the transaction. If it's real, then they can make money on the deal. See, they're already prejudiced to want it to be real so they can make money. They'll test it to make sure it's real, but they're already leaning one way."

"How expensive is it?"

"Twenty K. Perhaps thirty. These things are common but the images on them are special. A lot of people made themselves incredibly rich selling this stuff to chumps who don't know anything about antiquities. We have to buy them back as soon as everything is solved."

He shows Barry another vase. "This was a lot of hard work. I had to destroy three good copies before I made one that's obviously bad."

"To sell?"

"No one can sell it. It's clearly phony."

"What was it for?"

"I showed it to Adler so he'll see what a sucker I am. Right away he knew it's a silly forgery, and he must have thought it's dead easy to fool me. Lowell wants me to appear a pushover, not an expert. We have to get Adler to sell me an expensive, very expensive, item from antiquity." He points to the Orpheus he's working on.

"But Adler's legitimate. He won't deal with fakes."

"Two-faced Janus. If my rational mind is correct, he wants to unload something else, and perhaps he could make a real killing on both. Lowell is trying to squeeze him financially so he'll want to deal."

"You're throwing the net wide but aiming for Adler. What are you after?"

"The Samos vase is the key. It's the only thing outstanding from the heist. The gates of Janus remained open for two hundred years. Augustus closed them when he won the civil war. That's where we get the name January."

"If you get the real Samos vase, Imogen will be all over you."

"You may need to save me."

"And this Orpheus you're working on will be your key?"

Paris picks it up and holds it at a distance. "It's almost ready. We can't buy directly. We want to go through a certain third party. Can you make up a story of how your family wants to sell it?"

"My family?"

"From Sicily. Don't you have long lost relatives there?"

***

That evening Dr. Adler is having an invitation-only opening for an artist. Paris arrives and sees three or four dozen well-dressed people holding wine glasses, chatting in groups of three or four. Occasionally someone looks up at the paintings. In the middle of the room a group of people are picking at an hors d'oeuvres table. Two servers in uniform take around trays of jumbo prawns and prosciutto-wrapped melon. Paris passes on the hors d'oeuvres since he knows that on average they are handled by five different sets of hands.

He reminds himself to remain elegant, aloof, confident. An attendant takes his mohair coat as he begins sauntering, glancing at the art. He sees out the side of his eye a group of four chatting away but sneaking looks at him, and their speech suddenly comes from under their breath. He's sure they're talking about him, perhaps that he's acquiring questionable art with a bottomless pit of money. That's exactly what he needs, to be talked about, and to be talked about badly. It's better to be scorned than respected. The righteous never make news. That's what Isabella experienced, and it propelled her forward.

He overhears someone say, "If I had money I wouldn't waste it on this stuff."

A server brings Paris a tray of wine, and he takes a glass, sniffs it, then holds it like an English lord would hold inferior brandy. Dr. Adler sees him and comes over. They're gallant toward each other from the start.

"A pleasure that you honor my party with your presence. Do you like this art?

"Honestly, it doesn't agree with me." He takes up the tone of an English lord administering disdain.

"Honestly, neither with me, but a friend of the artist is a friend of my nephew, and I couldn't say no."

"It means a lot for an artist to have an opening on Newbury Street in your gallery."

"It triples the price of his work. An unknown becomes an overnight celebrity."

"When they're known, they're sought after," Paris says.

He stays above the common like an English aristocrat with his nose in the air. He's met lords when he studied in Cambridge, heard about the lord who dispatched his daughter to boarding school, as lords do, only to see her on Easter and Christmas. Each year the headmaster requested that "my lord" visit the school, until finally he assented. The staff were thrilled showing him around, "my lord" this and "my lord" that. He met his daughter at the end, sat in a gentleman's chair and said to her, "Dreadful place. I shan't come here again."

Paris must be alert, not screw up and say something that reveals his past. He has to remain ambiguous about how he got money for his art purchases. He should keep his past as mysterious as Adler's. It might be OK for people to have a vague idea that he's been in prison. It would be good for Adler to have a hint of that, perhaps let slide that he became a millionaire through white-collar crime. Women would run to him. News stations would line up for interviews. Prison endows the rich with celebrity status.

"Every artist is desperate to get shown in a place like this," Adler says.

"People follow the herd. An expert declares it's good, and people accept it."

"Isn't that the distressing way society is headed? Today's youth don't care about real art."

Paris continues decrying the way of the world, especially how young people are going astray. From Aristotle to Prince Charles, gentlemen have bemoaned that youth are cheapening society.

"I'm sorry to engage in business here, but I did find some news," Adler says.

"We always need to make room for business."

"I heard about an item that might interest you—a well-preserved statue of Apollo from Caesarea."

"You know how much I need Apollo statuary for the school. It wouldn't be complete without it."

"I went to see it in Philadelphia, and I was impressed how well-preserved it is, as if it didn't have a nick on it. Twenty-two hundred years without a nick. I can't even do that with the marble table I have in my entryway."

Just by the description, Paris knows that it's not a forgery. No forger would create objects that look nice. They would have cracked it here and there, worn down the images and added nicks, fading parts of it as if it was buried on its side for centuries.

"How fascinating. That's just what Pythagoras would have had in the center of his school. Not only was Apollo the god of light, but also lord of music and singing, and for the Pythagoreans, music meant mathematics—numbers are the perfect world."

"The best thing would be for you to travel down and look at it. If you're interested in having it, I'll negotiate a price."

"Immediately. I'll go down and see it personally."

"By the way, have you thought of making a donation to the Gardner Museum? I know it's rude of me to ask, being a long-time trustee, but I thought you'd like to consider it."

"I'll be thrilled to write them a check."

***

It's the first week in January. Barry is carrying a package in his suitcase as he rides in a taxi from the Palermo Airport to a hotel on Via Roma. It's the first time he's been out of the country, and he's fascinated as the taxi drives through Palermo's narrow streets. He had expected to find Sicily short-sleeves weather and is surprised to find that he needs a coat. He checks into the hotel and then wastes no time taking another taxi to the address of an art dealer, practicing his story en route.

He climbs the white granite stairs, worn in the middle from centuries of use, to the second floor and rings the buzzer. A female attendant lets him in.

"English?" Barry asks.

The woman gives him a mixed shake of her shoulders. "A little."

"I'm here to see Signora Bellotero. She is expecting me with a consignment."

She goes to the backroom and then returns, waving her hand for Barry to follow, which he does.

A respectable-looking businesswoman is sitting behind a desk, dark, matronly, shrewd face, large hands, clothes that probably used to fit but are now bulging with small cushions at the sides. Barry makes her acquaintance, and she gestures him to sit opposite her. He puts a package on the desk in front of her. She opens it and finds the statue of Orpheus that Paris made. She examines it with a magnifying glass while Barry looks at her.

"This is nice. Very nice."

She puts it on her desk.

"Are you in the art business?" she asks.

She speaks good English, accented. She's proper and polite.

"I work in information technology. This is from my old family home in Messina. Half the family left for the US in the 1920s."

This isn't a lie. His grandfather talked lovingly about Sicily, about fruit trees, the sun, the Mediterranean. If it was so great, Barry once asked him after listening to the same stories, why did you crowd on a cattle boat and leave?

She says, "Almost everyone here has relatives in America."

"My cousins phoned me last week and asked if I can help them appraise and sell this statue. They were afraid to contact you directly. They are afraid that people will know they have something valuable. This statue was hidden in their house."

"That is reasonable. Italians are afraid of the government knowing they have money, or they'll be taxed. In Sicily we also have to worry about certain powerful people knowing we have money."

"The mafia?"

She tips her head, neither yes nor no. "Do you live in New York?"

"I'm from the Midwest. I phoned my friend in New York, Joseph Contare, who deals in modern art, and he phoned you then put us in touch."

He is totally engrossed in his story. He knows that Paris selected her because she's legitimate but has tentacles with dicey people. Paris figured that she would deal with the vase even if she knew it was fake, as long as she could keep the transaction covert.

The woman begins rattling off a list of her relatives who live in America. She then looks at the vase and says, "We don't get much call for this type of art. I'm not sure how quickly it will sell."

"The family isn't hard up financially, but no one wants it. I sort of remember my grandfather talking about it. He said it's very old."

"Do they have expectation of its value?"

"That's why they called me. They don't know. They didn't even know if it has value. They sent me pictures, which I took to the Field Museum in Chicago. A curator thought it was famous, came from Southern Italy when the area was Greek. He estimated it was from 550 to 500 BC.

"I agree with him. I think it may be from Croton or Tarentum, two powerful towns on the southern Italian shore, what we call Magna Graecia."

"My friend and the curator thought that a person such as you can both appraise and sell it."

"We first need to authenticate."

He raises an index finger as if suddenly remembering. "The specialist at the Field Museum told me that there's an authentication expert on the East Coast of the US." He takes out a folded piece of paper and reads Dr. Ernesto Adler's name.

"Of course. Everyone knows Dr. Adler. A wise idea. I'll ask his services."

"I'm sure the family will reimburse any expenses."

"Do you know how the family got it?"

"It's been with us for generations. No one has an idea when or where. They're a business family now, lawyers and dentists. None of the young people care about it, so they agreed to let it go. Both Mr. Contare in New York and the

Field Museum curator said that it would be better to work through you rather than go to auction since the interest in this item is limited."

"I have contacts all over the world. I will advertise this item once it's authenticated, but these kinds of objects are difficult to sell because Magna Graecia is not popular with buyers. Most want Roman or Etruscan art or popular items from the great cities of antiquity. But the right buyer will emerge. My secretary can draw up a consignment contract in English, and I'll be in touch with an appraisal as soon as it's authenticated. Of course, what it actually sells for may be different."

"Mr. Contare said that he would almost guarantee that a buyer will appear as soon as word gets out that it's for sale."

Barry believes that she gets the hint. She knows she will be rewarded for her work.

Chapter Thirteen

Lowell travels to Miami and takes a room in Little Buenos Aires, the North Beach part of Miami Beach that has become home for many Argentinean expatriates. It's not as hot and humid as he had feared, so he doesn't have to worry about overstimulated saliva. He ate peanuts on the airplane and wrote down the time. The body does not break down corn or peanuts, so they are used as a marker food to see how much time the system takes between input and output.

He makes appointments with a string of shady characters from the list the commissioner had given him, hoping one will know something about how to squeeze a Cayman Islands bank account. Each crook gives Lowell overblown stories about their connections to Cayman Islands banks. He puts his hand on his belly during each account to gauge his alkalinity balance and dismisses all as duds.

Until he meets Little Mouse.

It's clear how he got his name: a short, stubby guy no taller than five foot two, sporting a mustache under a pug nose and two beady eyes.

"Some people call me Little, and some call me Mouse," he says to the lieutenant as they sit in a café on Collins Avenue. "Take your pick."

"I'm trying to squeeze a bank account."

"Everyone is trying to get their hands on those banks. Whose account is it?"

"I'm not sure. I only know I want it frozen."

"What's the bank?"

"I don't know that either. I only have an account number."

Mouse sits a little too still for a few seconds. "The Cayman Islands have three hundred banks. It has more businesses than people. Really. Every other hedge fund is located there. How am I going to find one in nine hundred thousand accounts?"

"That's all I got—a bank account number—and we want to get them to freeze it."

"The banks won't do anything for you. The movies are full of gadgets that break into accounts, but that never happens. You may be able to organize a denial of service, but that only lasts hours. If you're a cop, why don't you get your department to do it?"

"If I could I would. They would probably come to you anyway. How hard would it be?"

Little Mouse leans back but doesn't lose his intensity. "All depends if it's an account that gets used a lot."

"I imagine that all accounts are accessed from the US."

"Or Europe or Russia or India or wherever people want to hide money. Accounts go through the Internet. Routing through the Caymans is a formality. They handle billions of dollars a day. It's like the banks flip the finger at the rest of the world. Every criminal gang has an account there. Every dictator, drug runner, arms dealer, spy agency. The banks have offices in St. George, but that's decoration. A lot of the banks don't have a single employee in their office. Everything is done with bank encryption. No one can hack it."

The two remain focused on each other, not paying attention to the people walking past to the counter.

"The whole system stinks to high heaven." Lowell feels his throat constrict from the injustice.

"No one is going to stop it because those who have the power to stop it also have accounts there."

"How can I prevent this account from being used?"

"You have to offer compensation to someone inside, plus my commission. We can't make a withdrawal, despite what you see in the movies, but we may be able to place it on hold."

"How much?"

Little Mouse's eyes never waver off Lowell. "All depends. How long do you want it closed?"

"A few months."

"That's impossible. If we find the bank account, a month will be all we get. Account status reset every month, but the owner won't know that. We'll arrange an electronic notification that the government identifies his account as linked to organized crime and that he has to present himself to the local authorities to claim the account, and I imagine that your guy doesn't want to do that."

"Let's see what a month can do."

"How much cash is in it?"

"I don't know."

"You're not exactly overflowing with information. Costs a hundred grand. Fifty percent down. That goes to the guy who does it. The rest you pay if it's successful."

"I have someone in Boston who will pay you. What will you do?"

"First I have to find the bank. I'll run through each of the two hundred eighty-seven banks and see if the number you give me could be one of their account numbers. That should dwindle it down to a couple dozen. Then we have to try it one bank at a time, one code at a time."

"Let's start now."

***

Paris is among floor-to-ceiling shelves of books and documents in an obscure back room in the Massachusetts Historical Society library. He finds a Boston University dissertation titled *Falsified Paintings and Sculptures, 1900-1950.* He takes it to his laptop and begins inputting information.

He examines another book that has an article on recent archeological finds from the Pentapolis, the five Greek cities established in Libya. The area contains exquisite art which remains well preserved because of the aridity of its desert location. One of the paragraphs sounds familiar to him. And then the second. Perhaps he's tired and losing track. Where had he read this before? Then he remembers: he had written those two paragraphs himself as a graduate student, when publishing was so important to obtaining a position.

Someone had plagiarized his two paragraphs without citation. At one time he would have been incredulous, but now he just laughs it off. What does it matter?

"I'm swimming between bigger fish now," he says under his breath.

But is he? Is he falling into an old pattern that spurns success and taunts danger? Shouldn't he quit now, build his Pythagorean school and leave the rest to Lowell? He remembers attorney Rothman's warning about the fate of those who suddenly acquire wealth.

Get real, Mister Cool, he says to himself. You and James Bond have as much in common as a superspy and an opinionated, nerdy scholar.

He doesn't have one logical reason to continue down this path. He should stop his crude fixation on Adler and build his dream museum. He looks at his watch and then walks quickly to the Union Oyster House near Faneuil Hall. He's happy to see Barry arrive. Barry is one of those cheerful creatures who doesn't demand a lot out of life, so they revel whenever a high wind propels them onto a new shore. Barry is beaming from his trip to Italy, relating in a quick voice four or five incidents of the journey. Paris can see that he loves what he's doing now. He must never put Barry in danger. Barry ended up in prison because he refused to rat and took the whole rap himself.

They enter the restaurant and start with an order of a dozen oysters. Paris congratulates Barry on his successful trip.

"Best ten days I ever had. I drove up to the volcano while it was smoking."

"Mount Etna?"

"Yeah. Other end of the island. Every night was a different restaurant. And beautiful women. I thought I'd see a bunch of short fat peasant types who don't shave their legs—at least that's what I saw in pictures my grandparents had—so I didn't expect much. But those Sicilian women know how to move. I might not come back next time."

Their order arrives; they both dig in.

"No need to be a gentleman here," Paris says. "They're nice and fresh."

"They're better with lemon."

They eat oysters and sip beer in the loud, touristy bar; a wrapped painting sits on the chair next to Paris and two platters of oysters are on the table.

"How was the woman who's taking our consignment?"

"Sophisticated lady. She phoned before I left for the Rome airport to say that Adler will arrive shortly. Another fellow from Milan flew down and was real excited by the piece, identifying it right away as the long-missing Tarentum Benedetta Orpheus."

Paris recalls the first time one of his pieces was given to a scholar to authenticate. Paris stayed home all day worrying what the fellow would say.

"That's exactly what we want: the excitement of identifying a treasure lost for centuries. The exhilaration blurs your vision so that you don't think of its authenticity."

"She said that the buyer does more sophisticated tests on purchase."

"I'll take Dr. Adler's expert word. Did she give you an estimated value?"

"She said it's worth a lot because it's famous, several hundred thousand, perhaps a million."

Paris has another hit of doubt about the whole thing. A million dollars is a pretty big fraud. Will he get caught before he has a chance to undo everything? How will he be able to explain his actions? Is he Odysseus the great warrior or a prissy academic?

"She wants to consult other dealers," Barry says. "She agrees that it would be better if she sold it rather than it go up for auction."

"Naturally."

"How much do you think it's worth?"

"No telling. Art is not rational; even more removed from rationality is the price of art. Those experts will set a pretty high price for a famous lost piece. The more expensive it is, the more her commission. I put in three solid weeks working on it. I did two others that were good, but this one tops them all, by far the best antiquity I ever made. Maybe it should go in a museum when we're done. Other copies are in museums even though people know they're not real. Even if the museum has the real one, visitors might only see a display copy."

"How long before Adler approaches you about it?"

"He'll want to make the deal as soon as possible so others don't have a look at it. Although it's the best thing I ever made, I trust that Adler will spot it immediately."

They move on to scallops.

"I gave Lowell a hundred K to take care of a bank account that's possibly Adler's. He couldn't get the money otherwise. He'll let me know if it's successful."

Paris takes out a package from his briefcase.

"Is this the next one for the delivery man?" Barry asks.

"After you relax and refresh, can you take the train down to New York?"

"Yeah. What is it?"

They both talk with their mouths full.

"A small statue of Emperor Claudius. It's real, museum quality. I bought it at an auction and am selling it for ten K more. A gallery in New York has a client in Texas who's starting a collection."

"They'll both need our services."

"The ten K is yours. Don't forget to count the money. You can't trust people who deal in art."

***

Paris and Dr. Adler are making small talk in the center of the under-construction Pythagorean school. Adler had phoned and said that he wanted to chat. He had no urgency in his voice.

Finally, Adler says, "Where's that wonderful Apollo of Caesarea you acquired?"

He stands and leads Adler's eye to it. "It's perfect; calls

to be worshiped just as the Pythagoreans worshipped Apollo."

Paris shows excitement for the granite statue, but it's a bogus enthusiasm. It doesn't belong in his space. The people of ancient Palestine weren't Apollo-cult enthusiasts like those from Magna Graecia. It shows in the lack of projection from the statue. Those who sang the hymns to Apollo radiated light, which they infused into their art. Paris feels the projection of a statue by concentrating on it, standing a few feet away and taking in the entire object. The Caesarea statue has good workmanship, and it's in surprisingly good shape, but it projects no spirit. He snapped up the piece to get a quick inroad to Dr. Adler.

Adler says, "Don't tell people that you only paid eight hundred thousand or I'll never make a living."

"It's nothing. Last year alone I made ten million."

"Speaking of which, I think you'll be interested in a piece I saw recently. You mentioned that you wanted an Orpheus from Southern Italy. I discovered a sixth century BC Orpheus from Tarentum called the Benedetta Orpheus."

Even though he knows Adler came to announce this, the mention of the object—the one he made three weeks ago and asked Barry to present to the Palermo agent—jars Paris. At that moment he becomes aware that he's in his big lie for keeps. There will be no turning back once he engages Adler in this pivotal transaction. He feels like an actor who can't get out of his role.

Paris makes a dismissive wave of his hand. "That's impossible. It's been lost for centuries."

"It turned up—I'm talking days ago—in a private collection from an old Sicilian family. It may have been in their attic for generations." Adler's voice is feigned detached.

"That's too great a coincidence. Are you sure it's not a forgery?"

Paris already has this line prepared. He wants Adler to praise it. Once he makes a verbal claim to its originality, he has to defend that claim even louder.

"I flew there myself and examined it. I wouldn't bring

it up if I hadn't seen it."

He notices that Adler doesn't answer the question as to whether it's a forgery—one less sin he doesn't have to answer for. He wishes he had Lowell's skill of letting his gut guide him. He pushes.

"You authenticated it?"

"Other experts examined it. They know by looking at it, though the owner can do chemical tests if he doesn't trust the experts."

Now he knows that Adler spotted it as a forgery, but he's still willing to deal with it, and his duplicity propels Paris forward. Paris's scheme would have no traction if Adler wouldn't be willing to swindle him.

"You can't be serious. The real Benedetta Orpheus? You can really get it?"

"For a price. I told the dealer not to show it to anyone until you see it."

"That's the most exciting news I've ever heard. I never even considered that piece because I thought it didn't exist anymore. It's the perfect object for here. Pythagoras went to exile in Tarentum after he left Croton, and that piece—which he might have had personally in his school, might have even commissioned the artist—went missing for hundreds of years."

"According to the Italian expert, the later Pythagoreans of Alexander the Great's time mentioned it. They were a secret sect, so he doesn't know when or how it went after that until we find it mentioned in the Renaissance. It was thought stolen during a local war between Sicilian families in the late 1600s. We'll never be able to know its complete history."

"And now the family wants to sell?"

"Young people don't appreciate anything but their cell phones."

Paris unleashes a fat smile. "Pythagoras would have put it in the west wall facing the rising sun."

"I can arrange for you to examine it at a gallery in Palermo."

"Immediately. I'll drop what I'm doing and fly right over. We can't allow anyone else to get there first."

"I'll ask them again not to show it to a soul until you see it. I'll have my secretary arrange a flight for tomorrow."

Paris nods, brimming with energy as he walks Adler to the door. Paris wonders again if his plan is idiocy. Soon he will cross a point where he doesn't have the luxury to be able to abort.

***

Imogen and Helen are walking around the large old European art room near the rotunda in the Museum of Fine Arts looking at paintings. They're dressed like businesswomen, and they walk from painting to painting. Although Imogen is the boss, she defers to Helen when it comes to art. A few other people are also walking between paintings. A young artist has an easel set up near a painting and is copying it with oils.

"I thought we might as well keep an eye on the competition," Imogen says.

"No such thing as competition in art. Other museums encourage people's interest in all the arts."

"Tourists just go to one—the big one. Actually, most tourists don't go to any."

"Do I detect fear that Paris's museum will give us competition?" Helen chides playfully, but Imogen is not at all in a playful mood.

Imogen moves to the next painting, and Helen follows.

Helen says, "Perhaps that young guy over there will produce better art than the original."

"When psychologists put million-dollar paintings on a restaurant wall, no one notices, or when a world-class musician plays in a subway station, everyone continues to walk past. But when a museum announces the unveiling of a new acquisition, even the same painting ignored on a restaurant wall, thousands stand in line to see it. You and I are as influenced as anyone else; experts direct us."

"They direct our attention. We can decide what we

like."

Imogen makes a skeptical face. "They didn't notice van Gogh until an expert roasted his work. Art authorities are like shills in a three-card monte, getting everyone else to fork over money. Suddenly, by his validation, a certain art form becomes elevated, coveted, in fashion. No one questions an expert. If one person who's full of himself announces its artistic importance, others demur. A lot of trash hangs in museums."

Helen realized that she will never change Imogen's mind. "Museums of every color and stripe exist. We each make our decisions on what's art."

"There's an insatiable market for stuff. Those with a commercial sense set up promotion, selling anything from antique coins to copies of Monet Water Lilies. When you go to an art fair and pass booth after booth, there may be only a couple of real artists."

Imogen takes a breath, moves to the next painting. "So, what new piece is Paris selling today?"

"He has a statue. A Greek ceramic used in Delphi."

Imogen's eyes roll. "I don't think you want to get involved with him."

"Why?"

"What do you know about Paris?"

"What does that have to do with the statue he's selling?"

"He's been dealing."

"There's nothing wrong with buying and selling art."

"It's another forgery."

"It was authenticated."

"By idiots. I talked to the Met. The antiquities director took a two-second look at it and said it was a fraud."

Helen turns away from Imogen and focuses on a painting.

Imogen says, "He's not as innocuous as he looks. He's been unloading dubious antiquities left and right. Lord knows where he gets them. It's all third hand so no one can catch him."

"Does Lowell know?"

"He doesn't seem to care. He's waiting for him to trip up and reveal his part in the heist. He's waiting for one good transaction to nail him for good."

"How do you know?"

"I can read between the lines of police talk."

They walk to the next painting and obliviously stand in front of a woman looking at it. She scowls at them—they remain oblivious—then she moves around them to look at it.

"Paris is completely underworld," Imogen says. "I never believed his story that he just happened to find the art. There's no question in my mind that he was involved in the robbery. It's in his blood."

Helen looks away again, hurt. "I was never supposed to be involved in the robbery. I never wanted anything to do with theft or forgery." She points at a painting by Gerhard Richter. "He burned half of the works he produced. That might explain why artists struggle in poverty."

"While Paris lounges in his marble villa."

                              ***

The evening Lowell returns to Boston, he comes to see Paris at his Pythagorean school. He looks around with his hands behind his back. He points to a bronze statue of Aristotle.

"You make it?"

"No. It's made by a modern artist. I don't know anyone who's faked an old bronze. One test on the metal, and you'd know when it was made. Anyone can make a mold and churn out bronze figures. But I like it. I like Aristotle. We got much of our reliable information about Pythagoras from Plato and Aristotle. They talked to Pythagoreans who founded schools all over the Greek world. Without these schools, Plato and Aristotle would not have been able to write half the stuff they did. The Pythagoreans were the first to figure out that the earth rotates."

"We managed to freeze the suspect's bank account. He'll get a message that his account has been put on hold by a government agency, but he won't know anything else. He has to ask to have it unblocked, but then he'll have to come forward, and we'll know who he is. They'll be tax consequences, criminal charges."

"That's exactly what we need."

"One problem: it will reset itself in a month. The owner won't know that. He'll think that the authorities found his money, and he'll conclude that the account is permanently frozen."

"We have to rush. He'll be in a panic."

"Remember, we don't know for sure who it belongs to. It's a long shot."

"If our prey becomes desperate, we'll see him anxious to settle our deal as soon as possible."

Lowell walks around picking up objects and looking at them.

"Are all these real?"

"Real is a vague word. What's it matter when they were made? You like them? That's what matters."

Lowell gives a non-committal shrug. "I see that you just got back from Rome."

"Palermo."

"Mafia?"

"There's a special piece of art that I had to look at."

"Is it a piece that I may have already seen? As in right on this table?"

"It's been lost to the world for centuries. Then suddenly appeared, and just happens to be the ideal piece for a neo-Pythagorean school. Adler vouches for its authenticity—sort of."

"How much do the people in Italy know about it?"

"I'm not sure. Adler arranged for me to look at it in isolation, so I'm not supposed to know who's selling it. I'm not sure if he told people it's a fake."

"How long did it take to make it?"

"It made itself. We have a description of it from the Renaissance, before it went missing, but no one has a drawing of it. Based on that description and my research, I knew what it was supposed to look like and made a plaster copy of it for Apollo Self Storage. When I started working on the one that's now in Palermo, my work ceased being forgery and became art. I was sorry when it went away because this is its home. It's real to me."

"I see. You reckon that this will lead you to that Samos vase?"

"No promises in art."

He leads Lowell to the four vases in the section he has planned for Samos.

"This is the complete collection of vases. The last one—a copy of the missing vase—Helen gave me. The other three are original."

"This is your key to Adler?"

"You might see a big fish swimming around the bait soon. You have to yank me out of the water before he swallows me up."

"I'll give you a vial of potion to pour down his esophagus, so he'll spit you out. That's my area of expertise."

Chapter Fourteen

First thing next morning, Paris is listening to Gluck's opera *Iphigenie auf Tauris* while sitting on the divan in his temple dressed in a Versace robe and Kenneth Cole slippers. His surveillance cameras tell him that he's about to have a visitor. The door chime rings, and Paris puts down his book and shows Dr. Adler into the room.

"I have good news for you," Adler announces.

"You have the Macedonian Mercury and Psyche?"

"My word, you do ask the impossible. Next you'll want the Venus of Milos."

"A man like you can make the impossible happen."

"My colleague in Palermo tells me that you've spent a lot of time with the Benedetta Orpheus of Tarentum."

"Beautiful."

"They say that you showed a lot of excitement about it. My client doesn't want anyone to know the family who's selling it."

Paris gestures around him. "The secret is safe in this holy temple."

"It naturally belongs here with you. This is an Italian dealer's certificate of authenticity, but your authenticity is better than anyone's."

Paris, being distant, doesn't look at the certificate or listen to the false flattery. He knows that Adler takes him for a chump.

"Your word is all I need—mutual trust."

He hands Adler a short blurb about the piece written on a leather-bound pad that has an attached pen.

Paris says, "I can see on your face that it will be expensive."

"It's a better investment to pay a high price for a special piece since it will be appraised exponentially higher in the future."

"May I offer you a drink?"

"Such a shame that our love of art has to be contaminated by business. It's early to drink, but if you have one so will I."

"Gentlemen should never dispute about money," Paris says.

Paris walks to where the four Samos vases are displayed, drawing Adler toward them. Each is on a small pedestal, the one copy that Helen gave him and three others that he sought with determined energy. Paris picks up a bottle of whiskey and holds it up in front of the vases for Adler to see. Adler comes over and nods his head at the whiskey. Paris lowers the bottle, and Adler sees the row of Samos vases. His face freezes. Paris can see his eyes focusing on the copy that Helen gave him. Paris passes a long silence, examining both movement and stillness in Adler's face.

Paris says like an old buddy, "This section is dedicated to Pythagoras's early years in Samos. We don't know much about him there, or about Samos for that matter, but this section attempts to give us a sense of where he came from."

Adler, concentrating on the vase, doesn't say anything. That look from Adler disperses a mountain of doubt, giving Paris the sign he needs to go forward.

"Ah, you're looking at the only fake I have." Another old-buddy line. "The other three are of course authentic, but I have to wait for the fourth."

"That's impossible, as I think you know."

"On the contrary, now is the best time to buy it."

Paris hands Adler a glass of the liquor. Adler absently takes it and sips.

"Getting back to the other matter of the Benedetta Orpheus of Tarentum," Paris says. "I'd like time to contemplate."

Adler rouses himself. Paris concentrates on Adler's pensive face. According to Helen, he doesn't know that the museum had a copy of it, and he must be wondering where and how Paris got it.

"Without doubt. You don't think that I would allow anyone to make such a purchase without spending a long time thinking?" Pause. Adler looks again at the Samos vases. "You want this section to be about Samos?"

It is an impotent statement. Paris tries to appear dismissive but is concentrating on every word, every gesture.

"I need all four vases. It's a crime to have this unauthentic piece in an authentic temple. It pollutes the entire edifice."

This is the first time Paris makes it known that he's after the vase. Adler turns his gaze from the copy of the missing vase back to Paris. He can almost see Adler stop himself from saying that the place is full of fraudulent pieces. Adler visibly shifts his demeanor.

"They told me in Palermo that you were excited about that Orpheus."

Repeating that statement shows how distracted he is.

"I'll let you know soon."

Paris shows Adler to the door. They're politely formal, shaking hands, business smiles.

"By the way," Paris says, "how much is it?"

"Only five million."

Paris closes the door, goes to his makeshift desk and picks up a book titled *Obscure 17th Century Reproductions*, a PhD dissertation by an art history candidate. Five million. He laughs. Perhaps he told the woman in Palermo it was a fake but will give her a pittance to keep quiet. The rest is profit. He may have even jacked up the price after seeing the other Samos vases. That's how you get to be a millionaire. Paris laughs again. Five million just happens to be the amount that Adler forked out for the reward. He doesn't know it went to Paris.

***

Lieutenant Lowell is sitting in his car when he sees Dr. Adler leave Paris's building. He sees Adler excitedly dial a number from his phone. The pen that Paris gave Adler upstairs has a microphone. Lowell hears him talking into his phone.

"Dear Imogen, I have exciting news. I think I might finally be able to track down the villain who robbed our beloved museum. Let's call it a cross between a coincidence and a suspicion. I'll keep myself attached to the situation and ferret out the scoundrel. I think I know how to expose him."

***

Lowell meets Imogen in the Fenway park area behind the Museum of Fine Arts. It's a brisk winter day. As soon as Lowell approaches she says, "Why don't you arrest Paris?"

"For?"

"The burglary. How else would he have gotten his hands on those paintings? You can't actually believe his story about a storage business that he didn't own?"

They walk a few steps. Lowell had a good breakfast and feels energetic. Glucose must have been well excreted from the small intestine into the bloodstream and stored in the liver.

"Let's say that I nab him and take him to the station. There would have to be a charge: the Gardner robbery, keeping the Gardner Museum's stolen goods, concealing evidence. Take your pick."

"Then by law he has to hand back all the money the museum gave him. No thief can profit from his crime."

"His name will be all over the papers. Arrests are public records. So are the charges. His arrest will be front page."

Imogen remains incredulous. "He's also been making forgeries, selling them to unsuspecting buyers. Isn't that crime enough to arrest him?"

Canadian geese are surrounding them. They don't fly south for winter any more, and they're not at all timid around humans.

"So you don't mind if his name becomes public? Think for a minute. Let's say you're wrong. It's possible, isn't it? If you're wrong, then you owe him another ten million. It's double or nothing. How do you do on the roulette table?"

"We should tell Dr. Adler that he was the one who returned the art. He loves the museum and knows everyone in the art world. He'll tell us what kind of person Paris is."

"I wouldn't tell him anything, if I was you. Just wait."

"Tell me, Lieutenant. Do you think Paris was part of the original robbery?"

"You seem to be following him closely. My hunch is that you don't want to nail him for dealing in forgeries. You want the ten million back."

"I want justice."

"As I said, you want the ten million. Keep watching him. Just you. If he was part of the robbery, he'll trip up some time, and then you come to me and tell me if you're ready to risk it. For now I'd say be happy with what you got."

He realizes that her anger at Paris won't subside until she gets her money back, which may complicate the bait. She doesn't suffer from stress—she's a carrier of it. He must keep her away from Paris before she messes up their plan. It occurs to him how well she and Adler worked in tandem in the past.

***

Paris's museum has lots more ancient art, including a row of terra-cotta figures, bronze statues, and Greek glass. Some are real, others fake. The four Samos vases are displayed on pedestals in the center. Paris is dressed in a white toga. Helen enters. She's not friendly.

"Has all this gone to your head? Our reward wasn't enough for you?"

Her tone hurts him, but he must not listen to Eurydice's plea however dismayed. The hero keeps silent and acts without a care for his own emotion.

"Last month I stumbled over a company and invested a half million when its stock was at seven. It's now at twenty-three."

"You've finally made your research methods materially productive."

Odysseus and Aeneas never let hostile words or their own feelings for women divert them from fulfilling their destinies.

As if he doesn't notice how angry she is at him, Paris

shows her a painting leaning on the wall. "This is my latest, and you'll be happy to know that I got it cheap."

"Why's that?"

"A Dutch museum wanted to get rid of it because they weren't sure where it came from."

"You mean it was stolen by the Nazis and bounced from one shady art dealer to another?"

"Not necessarily. It's been in the museum basement for years. They don't know where it came from."

Helen looks disgusted. "The Nazis had underground bunkers where they stored the tens of thousands of art objects they robbed from across Europe. We know how it feels to be robbed."

"I didn't rob, and neither did that museum."

"You astonish me. I had you all wrong. You're a fence for fake and stolen art. Were you always like this, or did our money change you? What is it with you? What do you want?"

"I'm fulfilling a dream that your reward—a gift from the gods—is making happen. Here—I want to show you something you'll appreciate."

Still playing dense, he takes her to the four Samos vases. She keeps his distance from him.

"The full collection. But you know the one you gave me was a copy, while the other three are originals."

"How did you ever get them?"

"I paid dearly. No bargain basement here. The first was cheap, a mere twenty K, but when word gets out that you want something, they ask the moon. The third cost an astounding two hundred thousand, but still a tiny fraction of my portfolio. I can't spend money as fast as I'm making it."

"You're underworld."

Her scolding is jabbing at his side, but he can't allow anyone but Lowell and Barry in on the plan. She'll want details, and she'll be even madder to discover he's gunning for their most respected trustee, or worse, she'll tell Imogen.

"Please, Helen, don't be hostile."

"I guess you want your hands on the fourth vase."

"Now you're speaking the impossible. Impossible in two senses."

"What do you mean 'two senses'?"

"I'm sure that when you get it back, you'll sell it for far too much."

"You know that our statutes forbid us from selling a single thing."

"We're being theoretical since neither you nor I have it."

Helen walks toward the door. She looks wounded. He begins to make a gesture to console her but stops himself.

She whips around. "You know every underworld character, and you deal with them all."

"Some art works are difficult to obtain any other way."

"And Tizzio? You deal with him?"

"Who knows? Don't be so angry. I only want what's best for this Temple of the Muses."

"I see. And when Tizzio sells you the vase, you'll put it right here and have a complete collection. Good-bye, Paris. You really disappointed me."

Paris opens the door. "Orpheus has to get it right this time. There won't be a second chance."

Helen leaves quickly.

When the door closes, Paris is about to cry. Not very James Bond. He has time to quit before he commits to the Benedetta Orpheus of Tarentum. Should he run after Helen and explain? Is his relationship with her another in the string of life events he screwed up?

***

Next morning Paris and Barry walk through Haymarket—the noisy, crowded outdoor fruit-and-vegetable market where loud merchants stand behind their tables yelling out prices in Boston accents.

Barry says, "We've pulled off a lot of shady deals, but we're not any closer to pinning Adler as the thief."

"The vase is the cornerstone. We're counting on its current owner wanting to get rid of it for a fat reward. And we're counting on Lowell to make him need the reward."

"What makes you think Adler would risk surfacing with the vase, assuming he has it?"

"He wouldn't risk it for a small sum like a million or two, but if the deal with the Orpheus you delivered to Palermo is contingent on the Samos vase, the sum would rise to six or seven million free and clear, which should be too good to resist."

"How are you going to tie the vase to the Orpheus?"

"I don't know."

They both stop walking.

"Say you won't do one deal without the other," Barry says.

"He said he spread the word about our cash offer for the vase, but you and I have heard nothing from all our contacts. I'm guessing he doesn't need to spread the word though his contacts because he knows where that vase is."

"But Adler's been trying to solve the crime. He's been after the thieves."

"Adler's been after the stolen art. Now the art has been returned, all but one piece. That missing piece is a worthless liability. I'm offering his only chance to unload it."

"He can destroy it. It might be too much of a risk to have it."

"An art lover would never destroy art," Paris says. "If the owner of the vase is also the owner of the account Lowell found, we'll have a desperate person ready to eat the bait with Lowell's hook in it."

They move among large housewives carrying loaded bags of produce or pulling stuffed, rolling baskets.

Barry says, "You want something besides catching the thief."

"The thief is a challenge for any scholar."

"As in—trying to outsmart him?"

"As in—comparing notes by two experts. I didn't grow up in the kind of house he did."

As he says that, Paris wonders about his ulterior motives.

"You're offering a scholarly exercise."

"A contest among classical critics. Adler shouldn't resist the chance to outsmart us. Where would you put your bet?"

"Let's see, you can buy and sell phony art, and so can he. He's been doing this for a long time, but then again so have you. I'd guess it's a toss-up."

"I saw Adler's face light up when he saw that copy of the Samos vase. He was stunned."

"He would be stunned just to see that vase, especially since he doesn't know that a copy was made. Why would he want to rob the museum? He's a trustee."

"He loves the museum. His record shows that he would do anything for the museum. The robbery came at a bad time for them. They were struggling, stagnant. After the robbery, Adler and Imogen helped make it one of the best private museums in the country."

"They were doing all they could to find the thief. Adler even hired independent investigators on his own. That would mean that he isn't the thief."

Paris nods, passes ladies pulling two-wheel shopping carts. "One thing I have going is that he doesn't know that I'm the one who returned the art. He doesn't even know I'm an expert in this field, a disgraced academic. I know him but he doesn't know me."

"That's probably true. Your past remains pretty obscure, but maybe you don't know him as good as you think. Imogen certainly knows him."

"Mystery," Paris says. "Adler keeps himself mysterious."

They stop at a stand selling cups of shrimp cocktail. Paris buys two, and they begin eating. Paris asks, "Find anything else interesting?"

"Yeah, I've been keeping track of an old girlfriend who dumped me. She just bought a vibrator online. Made my day."

***

The next afternoon, Paris and Adler are seated inside a Charles Street cafe. It's midwinter; the outside terraces are closed. A waitress puts warm drinks in front of them and walks away.

Paris sees signs of distress on Adler's face—or is that his imagination?—that Adler discovered that his account has been blocked.

"May I speak in confidence?" Paris says.

"Your trust is more important than all our business."

Paris thinks Adler really does believe that he's a big, stupid chump.

"It would be absolutely wonderful to have the Benedetta Orpheus of Tarentum, but as you now guess, I'm after a certain vase."

Without emotion, Adler takes a sip and then puts down his cup. Paris fixates on Adler's facial language but finds it without expression, perhaps too much without expression. He needs Lowell's animal nature to get a bead on Adler.

"And you know where to find it?" Adler stops for a beat. "Or perhaps you already have it and are trying to make it seem as if you got it through a transaction."

"Of course I don't have it. That would mean that I robbed the museum. How can you think such a thing?"

"But I heard that you're making other inquiries besides me."

"I'm offering good money for it." Paris looks around as if ready to unload a secret. "A million. It isn't even worth ten thousand."

Paris imagines Adler silently calculating. A million free and clear and a chance to unload a hot item. But a million is chump change. Adler wants the five million from the Orpheus.

"You must continue to look for it. The person who has it would be the one who robbed the museum. Offer as much money as they want—more than a million if that's what it takes to draw out and track down the scoundrel. Once we have him, you can get your money back." Adler raises his hand like an oath. "You have my word."

"You must keep our confidence," Paris says.

"Mutual trust. I will never betray our integrity." Exaggerated sincerity. "As a museum trustee I'll make sure you keep the vase if you can point us to the thief."

"I thought that the current owner must be a gentleman who appreciates art."

"He's a thief, a money-grabbing charlatan."

"I'm sure he's sophisticated. Why else would he want to keep that superb vase?"

"Money. Isn't that why the museum was robbed?"

"A smart bank robber keeps his money in the bank. A smart museum robber would invest in the museum. A person can be excused if they are not inspired by the Dutch masters, but who wouldn't love to see the lines of that Samos vase when the morning sun hits it? And did you notice the copy I have is in much better shape than the other three. Almost as if it was made to order."

Adler takes a sip. "I see you've been considering this."

"That's why I confide in you. You see, I promised myself that I wouldn't get anything else until I had the fourth vase, not even that wonderful Benedetta Orpheus of Tarentum."

Adler's face turns hard. "We must do the Orpheus deal right away. I'm not sure how long I can hold off other potential buyers by making it an exclusive opportunity for you. If other buyers come in, the price might be twice what it is."

"I need the fourth Samos vase. It's obsessing me. I admit it. It haunts me at night. You must get it for me."

"Sir, I would never get involved in such a thing."

"I should have never asked you. No, Dr. Adler, it's up to me—entirely up to me. I need to make my intentions known. I need to have the cash ready. I need to plan the transaction. No, Dr. Adler, the owner of the vase needs to do nothing. But I refuse to make another purchase until I have it."

As if receiving sudden inspiration, Adler says, "Let's vow to trap that wicked thief together."

"Of course." Paris too looks like he's just got it. "If we find an inroad to the vase, we could make our Benedetta Orpheus transaction from Palermo at the same time, giving the seller less visibility."

"How do you mean?"

"We make it known that I want the vase for an absurd sum. In order to protect the seller's identity we'll make the exchange at the same time as our larger transaction of the Orpheus. The owner of the vase doesn't need to come forward, just make it available when we make our exchange."

"What a good idea. Let's proceed with the Orpheus right away."

"Only if the Samos vase is involved. Make every effort to get it."

Paris isn't sure what's going through Adler's mind. Is it greed? Is it a desire to trap Paris? Is it a legitimate desire to find the art thief?

"I see now," Adler says. "The seller can hide behind our legitimate deal. No one needs to know who he is. If I didn't know you, I'd think you had a criminal mind."

Both chuckle like gentlemen.

"Full steam ahead," Adler says. "Let's arrange the Orpheus deal immediately."

Paris is noticing Adler's desperation to make the deal, and he is wondering—perhaps wishful thinking—whether Adler is worried about money. Adler would be desperate to make that Orpheus sale no matter what. There's millions for him free and clear.

Paris puts on a relieved face. "It would be delicious to have the real vase."

"But if it turned up in your house, how would you explain that?"

"The only thing more awkward than having it turn up in my house, dear Dr. Adler, is for it to turn up in your house."

    Adler laughs. Very uncool.

Chapter Fifteen

Imogen enters Helen's office and plunks down in the arm chair.

"Why didn't you tell me that Paris has the three other vases?"

"How would that change anything?" Helen says.

"He's a fanatic. I found out that he gave up a wife and academic career for crime. His world ended when Constantine the Great embraced Christianity."

Helen eases back on the chair to distance herself from Imogen's intensity. "What's it matter? We have everything back except the vase. What's it matter what Paris does?"

"If he was in on the robbery, then we paid a ransom to a thief. It's illegal—we promised we wouldn't reward the thieves—it would compromise us to the world. And we're keeping his identity secret, protecting him from Tizzio's vengeance. We're accomplices to his criminality."

"We paid a reward and got our money's worth. That's fine. Why are you obsessing on Paris?"

"He got ten million dollars, half from our finest sponsor. And now he might do something that could damage the museum, as he damaged the university he worked for."

Helen makes a surprised face.

"Didn't you think I'd check up on him?" Imogen says.

Helen is torn between asking more about Paris and not wanting to know more. She ended it with Paris, but she can't believe Imogen's accusation. Or she doesn't want to believe it. Going around Paris's back to know more about him feels creepy. She stands and walks toward the bookcase. "Don't you think I too know something about Paris?"

"I'm sure you heard that he wants to contribute to the museum. Put out an email to our trustees asking if we should accept his money. I vote no. In the long run, being associated with a questionable character would hurt us more than losing what he wants to donate."

***

The Esplanade, a riverfront park with walkways and benches and lawns, is full of runners, Rollerbladers, cyclists, and walkers, even in winter. Paris is seated on a bench with the Charles River behind him as Helen approaches. It's the first week of February but surprisingly mild. He stands; they sit after a cool handshake.

"The board voted not to allow your name on our donor's list. They don't know that you're the one who brought back the art. They just know your reputation of buying and selling questionable art, and they're sensitive about that."

"And how did you vote? Against me?"

"I can't let personal feelings influence my job. The museum comes first."

It's not what he wanted to hear. A great hurt rises up his back. He's completely alienated her. She, like his ex, has her limits. Is it all a mistake? Should he have left it to Lowell rather than play superspy 007?

"I understand. It doesn't matter. I'll give the money anonymously, if you still want it."

"I don't want your money that way. I want you to change and become respectable."

"Respectable I've never been."

"You never do anything the right way. You have to keep life at a distance, always outside this world looking at another world."

Paris bows his head. "Don't be hard. Give me a little time to put everything in order. That's all I ask, a little time and a little trust."

"Don't touch another fake antiquity. Stop dealing in the underworld."

"Don't you see? We're called to the underworld, and we can't make the mistake of Orpheus and Eurydice. Even Odysseus had to dive into Hades to seek the wisdom of Tiresius."

He has a dose of rational mind which tells him that there's no way he's ever going to get near the thief and his alienation of Helen will be permanent. All his notion of looking at Adler's face to determine what the man is thinking is bogus; he was never good at people to start with. In antiquity, people examined others' faces for signs of demons entering the body and causing disease and ill fate. It didn't work then, and they were probably better at people than he is.

Stop this nonsense, he says to himself. There's still time to explain to Helen and apologize. Tell her you're sorry. What's it take to say sorry? She's Agamemnon's daughter, kin to Ptolemy, whose family left to Europe before the renaissance. His idea of the thief's identity is outlandish. How did he commit himself to such a scheme that has already ruined a relationship with the most wonderful person he's ever met? It's hurt everything Helen stands for. He can see the pain on her face. She hasn't come close to him for a while. She doesn't engage him. Plus, this superspy stuff is taking him away from building his Pythagorean school, maybe permanently. It may bankrupt him and send him back to prison. On top of all that, he now has a terrible reputation as an underworld character. He blew his life as an undergraduate. He blew a good marriage. He blew an envious career. Now he's blowing this.

Helen looks directly at him. "Paris, why did I ever like you? You have no grasp of reality. You live in a different world, and you don't even know right from wrong."

He sees Helen looking at him with a mixture of compassion and aversion. Is he his own worst enemy, defiling every gift the gods bestow? Is he trying again to be an Alpha instead of accepting his station?

But he knows that Adler isn't straight.

"There's a way out of the underworld," he says. "It's silence. It lives in the shadows. I swore an oath." He can't get the right words out. He wants to tell her, but that would ruin everything.

"I may not be allowed to know your past, but everyone knows your present."

Silence between them. When she stands and walks away, he walks up to the Charles River, his feet on that soggy edge of the grass. He phones Alice, telling her in a few sentences what's been happening, the returned art, the reward, the rough outline of his suspicion of Adler.

"You're repeating the same pattern," she replies. "It will lead to another catastrophe."

"I swore an oath."

"What do you have on this respected trustee?"

"Well—"

"You've got nothing, don't you?"

"I saw in his face when he looked at the vase."

"Forget it. You're no good at gauging what people are like. You know that. Your indictment of this guy sounds off the wall."

"You're right. Absolutely right."

Alice is sensible and real. If he had listened to her before, all those bad things wouldn't have happened.

He determines to give up. Forget about Adler and the Orpheus he made. Throw out all the fakes in his museum and go full speed on creating the place of his dreams. Odysseus, a wrestler like Paris, sized up challenges before undertaking them. He foresaw the trap of the Trojan War and urged the Athenians not to go.

"It's finished," he says to the river. "I accept my place. I will not be like Narcissus who was destined to have a long life but became so enamored with himself that when he saw his reflection in the water, he fell in and drowned."

He's not going to think ever again about Adler. He takes a long breath and practices telling Adler that he's not interested in their dealings. He wants nothing more to do with him. That's it.

***

Until Adler arrives at Paris's place the next morning.

Adler looks like Atlas carrying the world on his shoulders. His gentlemanly demeanor is faded. Paris invites him in, and they sit inside the Pythagorean triangle opposite each other. Paris begins with a gentleman's conversation, moaning the drab weather, the lack of direction of young people. He brings a couple of glasses of juice and a bowl of fruit on a gold platter and sets it on a hunk of granite between them. There's a new ancient statue of Artemis just behind Adler. Strauss's opera *Medea* is playing in the background.

"I get this wonderful feeling every time I'm here," Adler says, though his face shows the opposite. "Even though it's only partly completed."

"The Greek style enhances the human experience, if it's genuine. Have you ever been to Caesar's Palace in Las Vegas? The place makes me laugh. You can only have a phony experience in a place like that."

"I echo your sensibilities."

Adler has lost his spark. Paris turns away from Adler's face. It's a face of pain. Perseus must not look at Medusa. Did Lowell make Adler anxious by strangling a bank account?

"I'll show you something real."

Paris goes over to a statue. "This was just a hunk of rock, part of a mountain. Then along came a craftsman with two simple tools—a mallet and chisel—and he gave it life. Look at how it breathes, moves, feels."

"It has a flow, a balance."

"Only real art can produce that feeling because it contains the inner feeling of the carver. He gave it his own soul."

"Copies are detestable, a filthy part of this business," Adler says.

"Oh, I forgot that we were talking business."

"The truth is that for all of us, including you, art and business merge."

Paris believes that he has the upper position once again. Adler is in as much a state of need as a beggar with a cup in front of a convenience store. Adler takes a change-of-subject breath. "The Benedetta Orpheus of Tarentum."

Paris wants to test Adler's anxiety level. His security system is recording every movement, so he can re-examine the scene later. "I've been thinking about it. Of course it would be a good idea to have it."

Adler frowns in surprise. "You were massively excited by it."

"I'm really missing the fourth Samos vase."

"If we can't get it?"

"You made it known all around the art world that I'm offering a million for it. More. I must have it here. I must. Now you and I know that whoever has it shouldn't even be asking a box lunch. The current owner is only too lucky to find a cash buyer to allow him to recoup his investment. Let's raise the offer to two million. Money doesn't mean anything to me."

Does he see relief on Adler's face?

"I did spread the word, but no one has come back to me. It's in the art underworld somewhere. And although some of the people I deal with hear things, perhaps they're loath to work with a respectable dealer, especially given my position with the museum."

Paris can feel in his throat that Adler is lying. Maybe Lowell is right that we sense animal nature through different parts of our body. 007 never took anyone at face value.

Paris keeps piling it on. "That's why I need help from you—an honest and upright gentleman, a credit to the community, a man who's generous to charity, a pillar of refined taste and aesthetics. I need someone with high moral values."

"I'm glad you think well of my reputation."

Paris feels great sparring from the higher position. Because he has money and Adler needs it, Adler is extra solicitous. Is he being squeezed financially? Capitalism has a way of making one person in control and the other needy, though a man like Adler must never appear to beg.

Paris says, "There isn't a better place in the entire world for that vase except here. I must have it. Besides, it might help catch the thief."

"Anything to catch the thief." His voice isn't enthusiastic. "The thief, you know, still has the vase from the robbery years ago."

Does he hear confusion in Adler's voice? He hands Adler another small pad with a photocopy of the vase and a pen attached.

"Let's renew our efforts. Put out the word again. Let's ask the person who has the vase to think again. Two million."

"I'll put out another blast. Since the statute of limitations has expired, you'll get to keep the vase that you legitimately pay for."

Even Paris knows this isn't true. He wonders if the big fish is going to swallow him up whole. He needs to stay in rational nature. Like Icarus, he needs to get Adler closer to the heat.

Paris says, "Let's get back to the Benedetta Orpheus of Tarentum. You're interested in selling it for three and a half million, didn't I hear that? Remember, we're talking cash."

He sees Adler's eyes become animated. It's a lot of money that Adler can pocket and walk away with.

"Perhaps I can convince the owners to accept four and a half instead of five."

"What's a hundred thousand here or there among lovers of art? Shall we agree on three and three-quarters?"

"Quite right. Let's not penny-pinch. An even four if it's paid in cash. The owner prefers unreported cash. I think it's a fear of the Sicilian mafia."

Such a wonder of capitalism, Paris thinks. The trick of capitalism is to get people to need money. Then they'll lose their rational nature and do anything for you. When Paris passes someone on the street, neither even says hello, but if he enters that person's shop or restaurant, all of a sudden they are lifelong friends, anxious to help. They ask how you're feeling, wish you a good day. And they usually mean it.

"Cash is no problem."

Perhaps Adler will personally fly that cash down to open another offshore account in the Cayman Islands. Paris is wondering how much Adler will give the agent in Palermo.

Paris pretends to think. "Let's plan how we can make our transaction, which is fair and square, at the same time as the deal for the Samos vase. I'll have another two million ready. If we can convince the owner of the vase to use our transaction as a cover, it would make it safe for him to come forward with it at the same time and location as the transaction for the Benedetta Orpheus. He would never be in danger of exposure."

"I'll do everything I can for you. I'll get the word out again that someone is posting two million for the vase. It should come out of hiding and be sold this Friday at a location you and I agree on."

"I'll have the cash ready."

Adler says, "Take my briefcase. I don't have anything in it. You can stuff it with bills."

How convenient, Paris thinks, to just happen to have his empty briefcase that he wants to use. Adler really thinks Paris is a chump—hubris at work. He walks over to the window and hands Adler a glass of a concocted fruit juice he calls ambrosia.

"A toast."

"To art."

As soon as Adler's outside the building, Lowell once again turns on his receiver for the listening device inside the pen Paris gave to Adler. Again, Adler takes out his phone right away.

Lowell hears, "Imogen, we're going to have our big catch soon. I know the person who's transacting the vase, and believe me, he's underworld. I'm sure we'll catch the thief soon. You and I have been through a lot together over the years, but this will be the biggest deal. I'll come by and tell you all."

                                    ***

Helen hears the knock on her apartment and lets in Imogen, who's in a testy mood.

"I've heard that Paris has been trying to buy the missing vase."

"To go to any length to get the vase proves that he wasn't part of the theft. Otherwise, he'd already have it."

"It's all show. Look how he's making such a public show of wanting it. He'll say that he bought it but actually had it all along. He didn't want it to be with the other paintings that he just happened to find. No, he doesn't care about those but wants to keep the thing he likes. Finders keepers."

"He isn't an evil person."

"Stop protecting him. Lowell stumbled over himself to make sure he didn't reveal his identity. Paris must have tipped off the press that the art was returned so Lowell wouldn't have a chance to apprehend this phantom character who comes every six months. Isn't that why Paris is keeping his identity secret?"

"If he's known, the thieves will certainly come for revenge."

"Isn't it convenient that his identity wasn't leaked to the press? A group of thieves were in on the heist. Paris wanted out, and ten million is pretty good, especially if he doesn't have to split it."

"What about him running the storage place?"

"Come on. We both know who he is, but I know who he *was*. He has a record of deceit. I don't want to alarm you, but let's just say that there's a parole officer in between and he didn't buy the storage business by accident."

"He told me, but I don't believe he's evil. He's just gotten drunk on his money." She stands and walks around the room. "I just don't believe it."

"He knows every crook in the business."

"They deal with anyone with money."

"And it seems he has a lot more money than what we gave him."

"He's been dealing in art and trading stocks, making money as fast as he spends it."

Imogen's anger is spreading around the room. She's addressing Helen directly, but Helen is looking away.

"He lied to us about just getting into the art business. He's been in this business a long time. I won't tell you everything now. Paris was in on the original theft. I'm sure of it.

That makes our ransom illegal. He just can't hand over that last piece he stole, that Samos vase."

"Then the other thieves would be interested in him," Helen says. She's getting annoyed with Imogen's persistence. She never thought her boss would be so irritating. Why is she gunning so hard for Paris?

"Don't you see? He made sure that no one except us knows who turned in the paintings. We reveal his identity and he'll find a legal way to hurt us. See how he made it?"

A doorbell stops the argument. Adler enters bounding with enthusiasm.

"The thief is falling into our trap."

"Who is it?"

"The very man who wanted his name as contributor to our beloved museum."

Helen sees Imogen looking at her. Neither reveals emotion. Helen wonders whether Imogen will tell Adler who Paris is. Perhaps she already has. How is it now, after years of friendship, she doesn't trust her?

"I knew it," Imogen says to Helen.

"Are you sure?" Helen asks Adler.

"I was shocked. I knew he was dishonest the day he set foot in my gallery, but I never suspected. You know him?"

"We've both met him," Imogen says.

Helen quickly adds, "Because he wanted to donate to the museum."

"I admit that I encouraged the donation before I knew what the scoundrel was up to."

"What's your proof?" Helen asks. Her tone is logical, as opposed to Imogen and Adler who are expressive.

"He wants to pass me an expensive fake. I said that I'll take it only if I can get the Samos vase for another astronomical sum. I already made it known that I'm offering big money for it. He wants to trick me out of millions. And to think that he wanted to contribute to the museum. The nerve. I'm hoping we catch him with the vase, which would mean that he's the thief—one of them at least."

"Catch him with the vase," Imogen repeats. "How do you know the copy he has displayed isn't the real vase?"

Helen starts to speak but checks herself. Should she stay true to her promise to Paris to not tell anyone that she gave him the copy? Is she now an accomplice?

"I'm sure he has the real one hidden away," Adler says. "What I'll do is tell him that we'll make a deal for that vase at the same time that I buy one of the fake artifacts he's unloading for four million. I told him that I'll give him another two million cash if he brings the original vase. I'll bring the cash— six million—in my briefcase so he sees it. We'll nab him and turn him over to the police. I'll take my money back, and he can keep his fake statue."

"Great plan," Imogen says. "We'll finally have justice for the museum."

Adler puts his hand on Helen's shoulder, a paternal gesture. "It'll be over soon. I'll let you know exactly when you should step in and catch him."

Adler leaves.

Imogen says to Helen, "Maybe we should tell him that Paris got the reward."

"That's not necessary. Paris can stay in the underworld."

Imogen too leaves. Helen stands alone and agitated among the art of her living room. Whose side should she be on? She answers herself by saying that she should be on the side of whoever is telling the truth.

***

The next morning Helen enters Lieutenant Lowell's office, a semi-Spartan room—a desk with papers and phone, computer, two chairs. Helen greets Lowell who makes a gesture for her to take a seat in one of the chairs.

She begins. "I've been thinking that perhaps we've overlooked the most obvious."

"And where would that be?"

"Paris."

Lowell walks around, sits on the edge of his desk and

looks at her.

"I thought you two had become friendly."

"Perhaps that obscured my thoughts."

"When you're dealing with kidnapping or assault, it always ends up being relatives. What's your hunch?"

"I assume that the thieves knew that ten million was all they were going to get."

"Don't assume. Tell me what you *know*."

"I know that he's been obsessed with the Samos vase, or pretending to be obsessed with it. If it should fall into his hands, he could say he bought it trying to get the thieves, but like that thug who supposedly appeared in his storage unit, it disappeared. And the most important thing is that we don't know anything about him."

"I know everything about him."

Helen isn't surprised by the revelation.

Lowell continues. "Would it change your feelings if I told you he's got a prison record?"

"He told me. Imogen told me. He said he's ashamed of his past."

"How about that he was sentenced for art forgery?"

Helen tries to control her hurt. She composes herself. "Do you know he's doing it again?"

"I don't only know; I help him."

"How? I mean, why? I mean, when?"

"He's all I've got to get the thief. If the thief is his friend or enemy, he'll come to Paris."

"Then you believe him?"

"Do you know why people talk about the heart as the seat of emotion? We draw all these heart-shaped images for love and romance."

"I beg your pardon?"

"You see it in all the stores now right before Valentine's Day, hearts and arrows, but love and romance exist in the brain. The brain doesn't look like it does anything—it just sits there. Until the 1700s, people thought that love and romance resided in the heart, which we now know is a tough pumping muscle. The heart is always active, and if you look at it from a primitive perspective, it looks like it controls all aspects of life. Who would have suspected that it's all in the brain? They couldn't see ions flowing down neurons and synapses discharging. They were captivated by the heart because it's always working. The spleen and liver and kidneys are active as well, secreting and pulsing, changing the food we eat into blood and nutrients."

"I'm sorry, I don't understand how this relates to Paris."

"You have to understand the body if you want to understand the brain and vice versa. Before microscopes, no one thought the brain did anything."

"And Paris?"

"Paris is pulling off a lot of shady deals. Like the brain, there's a subtle action behind the scenes. He didn't want me to tell you about his past, but this saga is building up in the ascending colon, ready to come out any time. He's trying to get to the thief, or he's the thief himself. Which do you think?"

"I thought we're not supposed to know about him."

"You think I just sit around writing reports? You and Imogen know a little about him too. She traced his ex-probation officer, who stonewalled her, as I asked him to do."

"She's concerned that we gave ten million to the person who robbed us. She's got it in for Paris. What's your conclusion about the theft?"

"It seems that the person who had the art isn't the one who wanted it stolen. I think I managed to squeeze a suspect bank account. This might precipitate panic and force him to make a foolish move. It's a long shot, very uncertain. Meanwhile there's a big cash offer to buy the missing vase. Why do you think Paris bought the storage unit, given that he's a professor?"

"He couldn't go back to teaching. He wrote articles about ancient sewer systems." A pause. "At least that's what he says."

"How do you explain breaking and entering?"

Helen is about to speak but stops.

"I met his ex-wife," Lowell says. "She hasn't let go of him even though she divorced him. She gave me an article he wrote against the Church."

"Oh, he looks down on Christians."

"Don't worry, his info won't get out. Paris is now fully engrossed in the art underworld. He just mortgaged his museum, which means that he's playing for keeps. When we catch someone with that vase, we'll know that person was in on the heist."

Chapter Sixteen

Helen is walking down Newbury Street looking at art galleries. She stops in front of the window of one and sees a salesperson pressing a sale on a couple. She walks to the next gallery where a salesman is standing next to a well-dressed older client, gesturing at the picture and talking away, he too obviously trying to convince the client to buy. She wonders when art became a commodity. Medieval city states tried to impress with art and architecture. They fought wars over saints' relics but they didn't buy and sell art as today.

She walks up to the next gallery, which is Adler's, and goes inside. It's empty and has the feel of being empty most of the time. Helen begins looking around. The sales clerk comes from the back room and approaches her with a salesperson's smile.

"This is wonderful," Helen says to the clerk. "Who's the artist?"

"Isn't he great? I love the energy in his work. What piece caught your eye?"

"Actually, I wondered if Dr. Adler is in."

The sales clerk discharges her sales tone and becomes friendly. "He's been here a lot these days, almost every day. Are you a friend?"

"We work together."

"There he is."

She points out the front window as Adler exits a taxi and steps up to the gallery.

"Ms. Muller, you should come by my gallery more often."

He's elegantly chiding, but she sees worry on his face. The clerk exits to the back room.

Helen points around. "It's invigorating to have a place where art changes. The museum has been the same for decades."

"But such an exquisite sameness." His voice is absolutely sincere. "I love the museum."

"I told the policeman who's handling the case about your suspicion."

"What's the policeman's name?"

"You'll meet him soon. Thanks to you, the police will be ready to trap him with the missing vase."

"I thought long and hard about how to catch that jackal Paris. The small transaction I'll be making with him will cost me money, but the real money I need is two million dollars cash for that Samos vase. He's protesting that he doesn't have the original, but we'll see that he's lying as soon as he sells it to me. I'm certain he has it and will produce the vase because he needs to get rid of it. Once we see it in his hands, we'll know he's guilty of robbing the museum. And we'll make him pay."

"Dr. Adler, you embody the museum in your work."

"You embody the museum in your life."

"What about the man who turned in the paintings? Don't the police know him?"

Adler still has no idea Paris returned the art. That means that Imogen didn't tell him. She's thinking of telling him herself but stops herself again.

"I too know him, Dr. Adler. I told the board that the person came to the police with the art, but actually he approached me and demanded that his identity remain secret."

"Where does this person live? I mean, certainly the police know."

"One thing at a time. The police will be able to tell you after we nab Paris with the vase."

"I'll tell you where and when to meet us. You bring that policeman. You'll find that scoundrel Paris with the vase and my six million dollars in my briefcase. Be sure to catch him when I telephone you."

"I'll tell everyone to come. The museum will have its money back."

"I'm at the museum's command."

"I hope to see you at the next trustees meeting."

"Please don't bring up past lapses. It's already a high-stress business. I come whenever I'm in town."

***

Soon after Helen leaves Adler's studio, Barry approaches the glass door of Lowell's office, knocks and walks in. Lowell looks up quizzically.

"I'm a friend of Paris."

"I know who you are."

"Paris's ex told him that he's going to get caught and framed and that he should immediately pull out."

"And his response?"

"There's a cafe on Airport Cargo Road called Frank's. Tomorrow is Valentine's Day. The place will empty in the late afternoon. If you meet me there tomorrow at five, you'll see everything."

Lowell nods as if Barry need not say anything else.

***

A scholar in a dim auditorium is delivering a painfully boring slide lecture about religious icons used in medieval art. More than half the seats are empty. Helen and Imogen are seated in the back row. When they see Lowell enter, they both discreetly go to a corner and speak silently to him.

"We're ready to go," Lowell says.

"How do you know?" Imogen asks.

"You know too."

"Dr. Adler has been keeping us informed."

"The guy who's been making all of Paris's shady deals made contact."

"You mean he's betraying Paris?" Helen says. Everyone is whispering.

"Why not?" Imogen says. "There's millions on the line."

"I'll pick you up tomorrow at four thirty," Lowell says.

"Dr. Adler said they're going to meet tomorrow at Logan," Helen says. "Cargo gate number four, at six in the evening. Dr. Adler is giving Paris a briefcase of money. He'll phone me exactly when there's enough evidence to incriminate Paris, which means finding him with the original Samos vase. He'll have the surprise of his life."

"The one thing I can say," Lowell says, "Is that there *will* be a surprise."

"The thief will be easy to spot; he'll be the one holding the vase," Imogen says.

"Will he lead us to Tizzio?" Helen asks.

"Or he'll have to take the entire rap himself," Imogen says.

The lecturer drones on.

***

Paris is in a rental car waiting outside the cargo terminal off Prescott Road near Logan Airport. It's a chilly St. Valentine's Day. Adler drives up and parks in front of Paris. They both get out. Both are wearing long coats and gloves like gentlemen. Adler has freight papers in hand. Paris takes Adler's briefcase out the backseat, and they walk together to the warehouse surrounded by a light drizzle. Workers are leaving for the day. Paris knows it's do or die, but he feels light and positive. Is he deceiving himself?

Adler stops in front of the door. "It cleared customs. It should be in that building."

Adler shows the papers to someone in the front office. He points inside the warehouse, telling him to look in section *D*.

Adler and Paris walk among shipments of boxes and small crates looking for that section. No one else is in the wide, open building.

"It's the ideal time to come," Adler says. "Between shifts on a semi-holiday." He points. "Section *D*."

Paris understands that Adler has done this before. So much for that upright gentleman image.

They begin looking at the cartons. Adler spots a box about four feet high with his name on it. He goes to the front counter and returns with a crowbar.

"The safest way to ship valuables is to send them as if they're worthless. I've never lost anything this way."

Adler stops and looks at Paris. "I'm sure you know the Samos vase is linked to the museum theft."

"Dr. Adler, your money is guaranteed. Who would have your interests in mind more than me?"

"I know what you suspect, but you have absolutely no proof."

"One hundred percent right. No proof at all."

"The die is cast. You can accuse me all you want. I don't care about your suspicions. No one will believe you. A man embroiled in the underworld versus a museum trustee who's dedicated two decades to finding the stolen art."

"How did you let all that art slip out of your control?"

"Traitors."

"A miscalculation?"

"Hooligans. Scoundrels. Villains." He points to the crate. "Would you like to open it?"

"Mutual trust," Paris says.

"To refresh your memory—perhaps I'm tricking you."

"Your word is all I need." Paris says.

Dr. Adler smiles, says. "No, I insist you open it."

It's the first smile Paris has seen on Adler in three weeks. Adler takes the crowbar from Paris's hand and begins to take off the top. Paris walks up and stops him.

"It's absolutely not necessary."

Adler stops. Paris takes the crowbar and puts it on top of the crate. He hands Adler the briefcase. Adler begins to open it but stops.

"It isn't necessary to count," Paris says. "Mutual trust."

"Of course. There isn't any need to open it." His voice comes out hoarse.

"You should."

"Your word is all I need."

A side door opens, and D. Jason enters carrying the Samos vase with both hands in front of him. He walks toward Paris and Adler. As soon Jason comes close enough to see

Paris's face, he stops cold, alarmed.

"Mr. D. Jason," Paris says. "I was wondering if I'd have the pleasure of seeing you again." He turns to Adler. "This fine fellow kept the stolen art at a storage business dedicated to Apollo." Paris shows no anxiety about seeing the big guy again, but he feels slightly worried.

Adler points to Jason. "Him?" He points to Paris. "And you."

Adler looks quickly at Jason and then at Paris and back again. He steps back as if he got slammed with a right hook. "You scum! Both of you. You both double-crossed me."

Paris says, "Dr. Adler, what a changed man you've suddenly become. We're now partners. You have a suitcase of six million. I counted it carefully. It's all Monopoly money, but I now have this fake statue."

"How do you know it's a fake?"

"I made it myself especially for you. Doesn't that make us even? I'm the one who created the Navarites."

"You're that professor? You went to jail?"

"Prison."

"You made all those antiquities?"

"I knew you'd spot this one as a fake. You're too good at what you do."

"You scum." Adler's voice becomes logical. "It all fits in place. I thought that ex-cop double-crossed us. You want to trap me."

"Let's not become melodramatic. No one can be against such a model citizen as you. I wouldn't dare soil your reputation."

"I love the museum."

"That was your downfall. You didn't want the museum infected with the Samos vase."

"How could you have known? You never touched it. This real one."

"Real is a generous word. The problem these days is that no one wants to do research. They skim over details, afraid to exercise their brain." He turns to Jason. "Perhaps you didn't notice that I had a plaster copy of this Orpheus at Apollo Self Storage."

Alder says to Jason, "And you—you pretended that you didn't know anything about the art. Who do you work for? Tizzio?"

"I don't know."

"He probably doesn't know what was in the crate," Paris says.

Jason shrugs.

"You'll get your reward all right," Adler says. "Both of you."

"Don't be too rash, Dr. Adler," Paris says. "If Jason works for Tizzio, he has long tentacles."

Adler points to Paris. "This guy is going to get us both. You go destroy him. No mercy."

Jason throws the vase to Adler, who catches it and puts it under his arm. Jason moves forward, thug grin, and grabs the crowbar. Paris notices Jason's overconfidence and laughs. Worse Jason grin; another Paris laugh. They prance around each other while Adler watches. Jason rushes Paris, crowbar raised. Paris takes Jason's wrist and adds to its downward momentum enough to spin Jason. The crowbar rolls onto the floor. Paris keeps a tight hold on the wrist and begins twisting it as Jason is squeezed to the ground in one smooth movement. Paris places his knee on Jason's side while turning the arm, pinning Jason to the ground as Paris did in the New Mexico bar. Jason lets out a groan of pain. Adler becomes alarmed. He picks up the crowbar with his free hand ready to go after Paris.

The side door opens; all eyes turn. Barry ushers in an inquisitive Helen followed by the determined Lowell with two policemen and Imogen walking behind them.

Helen steps forward and examines the frozen scene, eyes wide open, turning from Adler to Paris.

"Dr. Adler? Paris?"

Lowell points to Adler. "May I present the mastermind of the Gardner heist." He points to Jason. "And here is perhaps one of Tizzio's employees."

Paris lets go of Jason. The two policemen step forward. Adler drops the crowbar and lets out an uncomfortable laugh as he looks at the vase under his arm. Paris looks at Lowell, and Lowell turns his gaze to a video camera tucked away in the corner of the room. Everyone's eyes follow his.

"It's all recorded," Lowell says.

Lowell takes the vase from Adler's hands. A worse Adler laugh. Jason defeated on the floor. Paris, smug, reaches into his jacket pocket and takes out a pink Valentine's card, handing it to Helen.

Final Chapter

Helen is walking down the street in front of the building housing Paris's museum. She has a package in a shopping bag. She goes through the rough entrance doors and takes the elevator to Paris's floor.

She rings the door chime and enters, finding Paris sitting on his couch drinking wine out of a water glass. A bottle of cheap Gallo Burgundy sits on the marble table next to an open can of mackerel, a box of Ritz crackers, and a half-cut pack of Velveeta. He's wearing something similar to what he wore at the storage unit. Near the couch is the video camera on a tripod. The place is still full of dust and broken pieces of construction waste. The fresco that Helen commented on is missing, and another of his paintings is on the floor leaning against the wall. She puts down her package, looking around at the missing art and asks Paris the question without using words.

"The ballet asked me to donate it to them. Besides, it didn't match the furniture."

She turns her gaze to the bottle of Gallo and the chintzy lunch. "That's quite a climb down."

"A touch of nostalgia. I had to buy back all the fakes I sold. Plus, a university wants me to donate a million for a new classics program, so I need to save money. They're going to name a wing after me."

"And what name will they put?"

"I've gotten used to Paris."

"I don't know you as anything else."

"Paris, as in Helen. Remember?"

"She went to Troy voluntarily. Can I still call you Paris?"

"I wouldn't have it any other way."

"You can't imagine how many people we had outside

the museum's doors. The paper got it all right except Adler's identity."

"No one guessed a trustee who contributed to the reward. Would you like some cheap Burgundy?"

"I'd love some."

"How about Ritz crackers, mackerel, and Velveeta?"

"Sounds great."

"This is my world. I'm not suave. I'm not elegant. I screwed up childhood. I screwed up grad school. I screwed up being a professor. I screwed up marriage. I was so worried that I'd screw up a gifted ten million dollars."

She sits. He cuts her a thick slice of Velveeta and fishes out a handful of Ritz crackers and puts them on a napkin, an awkward romantic gesture. Sitting across from her, he doesn't feel like being Odysseus anymore.

"I ate this almost every day in grad school."

"I used to eat peanut butter with liverwurst," she says.

"Crunchy or creamy? Let me guess, you're smooth and creamy while I'm extra crunchy."

"You've got me all wrong. It's you who are sophisticated: literature, history, classical languages, opera.

The two sit silently until Helen says, "I first want to apologize."

"Don't worry about it."

"Apologize for not trusting you. I wanted to tell you that. I don't know how to say it."

"I didn't give you much to trust."

"I feel like a fool."

"A fool is the last thing you are. You're the nicest person I've met. I know that under that well put-together exterior is a well put-together person. You believed in me more than anyone else."

"Maybe you're right about that. Lowell has this uncanny sense. He gave you free rein because you were researching in a way the police couldn't."

"I was his bait, but he was always watching after me. More Velveeta?"

She takes, looks around. "What about the piece that I thought was stolen by the Nazis?"

"It's been researched, but no one knows where it came from. A veteran's society asked me to donate it, which will somehow purify it."

"Once one of those groups gets something like that, it sort of makes the art legitimate. After a year or two they can sell it at Christie's."

"My interest in collecting art has temporarily waned. A lot of what I bought doesn't belong here, but I bought it for another reason. I focused on Samos because Pythagoras was from there, and we were talking about the Samos vase, but it should be a temple to science, philosophy, and art."

They look out the window.

"You know, Helen, I didn't do this for money."

"I know that. I know that you don't care about money."

"I didn't even do it for the Gardner Museum. I did it because I wanted to make you happy."

"It's the nicest thing anyone's done for me."

"I mean, I just felt that it would make you feel good. I don't do much for others, I guess, but I wanted to do something for you."

"Thank you."

"I didn't want to be like Orpheus. He couldn't get Eurydice out of Hades because he vented his love."

Color rushes to Helen's face.

"Orpheus should have remained steadfast," he says. "That's the way out of Hades."

There's a charmed feeling between them.

"Are you going back to teaching?"

"All universities care about these days is being profitable. There's no room for people like me."

Helen picks up her package.

"I came to give you this present."

She hands the package to Paris who opens it, pulling out the Samos vase.

"No, no I can't..."

"The board was unanimous that you should have the original."

"It was only a game..."

"It belongs here, next to the others."

"Please..."

"You're the best person to have it. It was Imogen's idea. She stood up in the meeting, apologized, and gave you her full support. She wants our two museums connected."

Paris turns away from her, goes to a counter and produces a bag of jelly beans. He puts it on the table in front of Helen; that's about as romantic as he can get.

"I'm going to forget this idiotic Pythagorean school thing. No one's interested in the past."

"Oh, please don't. If you don't go through with it you'll be depriving the world of something important."

"You believe that? Really?"

"Don't sound surprised. Didn't you say that we need Pythagorean thought today?"

"I don't do things right. It gets me in trouble."

"I would be hurt if you didn't continue at full volume on this museum."

Paris thinks about this. "I may need a curator here. Would you take the job?"

"I would. And not just to thank you."

"It is Lowell you have to thank. He told me that working in the background is much healthier for a stable bladder. He found a way to squeeze Adler financially, and that made him desperate to make this transaction. He told me to live big, offer money. Otherwise, Adler would have never have risked coming out of hiding."

"It's startling that the man who directed the robbery of five hundred million dollars worth of art is free," she says.

"Because he too had money. He paid and walked, while a poor black kid five blocks from here robs a few dollars from a 7-Eleven and ends up in jail. That wasn't the Greek way."

"Paris, perhaps you idolize the Greeks too much. They had slaves and abused people just as much. The Athenians raped Cassandra."

Paris stands and starts talking fast. "Funny thing, the difference between an original and a fake. Lots of times we get so used to a fake that we think it's original. Could be an object or an idea. After a while we don't even question if we have an original or a fake. In the case of an idea, we believe we've come up with it ourselves. In the case of an object, we forget where it came from, convincing ourselves that it's an original, but how well do we know?"

He takes up the vase to eye level and looks at it.

"What are you getting at?"

"A guy from the University of Chicago just published an article that Archimedes experimented in the Temple of Jupiter in Syracuse. A full professor writes this trash. People don't research—that's the problem. And soon his off-the-wall idea becomes orthodox, accepted. But it is plain wrong. That temple belonged to the Stoics. Can you imagine Archimedes in a Stoic temple?"

He walks around and continues ranting. "Who cares if it's wrong? They're all dead anyway. Tittle-tattle becomes truth, like all that nonsense in travel books. Modern people complain about the ancients living on rumors and half-truths, but are we any different? No research. No study. You can know history by reading a survey book—five thousand years of history in one slim volume."

Helen furrows her brow, starts to speak but remains silent as he continues his tirade.

"Take this vase. We know it's original. No doubt about it. It's been sitting in the museum for a hundred years, the museum posted a blurb explaining how the museum got it. Who would question such authority? It's beautiful to boot. But look here at the foot of Iphigenia. What do we see? Why, what we would expect, a bust of Clytemnestra. She's wearing a chiton with a broach on her left shoulder. The Athenians did wear chitons, which have buttons in the center, and the Macedonians wore peplos with broaches on their left shoulder, but Athenians began wearing chitons like the Macedonians in the first century Before Catastrophe, a hundred years after the vase was supposedly made. And in Samos, no woman wore a chiton."

Helen looks closely at what he's talking about.

"What's a hundred years? All antiquity is the same, like there's no difference between 1860 and 1960."

"Are you sure?"

"No one needs research. Anything goes. But eventually, someone finds out."

"It's a fake?"

"As sure as Athena is a goddess."

Helen looks more carefully at the object and then she looks up.

Paris points to the other Samos vases. "There were these three vases over there, until an American collector went to Europe in the early 1900s. Respectable lady with an incredible eye for art. Suddenly a fourth vase turned up, and it looked good. An expert authenticated it, and it went for what was not a trifle amount of money."

"You knew all along?"

"The minute you showed me the picture. I figured that the thief must be an expert who can spot fakes, a connoisseur who wouldn't have mixed it with real art. Samos was an old civilization that gave us Pythagoras. Not many artifacts survive from it, so you can create a forgery pretty easily—dry out the clay and make the vase look old. I did it myself. There wouldn't be too much else from Samos you can compare it with. More wine?"

Helen is speechless. Paris refills both glasses.

"Dr. Adler loved the museum. He knew the vase was fake and didn't want the museum debased by it. He didn't think I knew since I never touched the original. He thought I was a dunce. Very bad to underestimate your adversary. He gave information to two unscrupulous individuals to rob the museum. Maybe they worked for the elusive Tizzio, maybe not. Only problem was that he trusted the thieves. They didn't give a hoot about art, as you know by how they acted in the museum, half-destroying the pieces, then running off with them."

They look at each other. A smile comes over Helen's face. Paris puts the vase in the place of its copy.

"It was a hunch. We had to get Adler to sell me the vase. It was like dealing with two different people—one art lover and one crook. Adler wanted to get rid of that vase which was like an impurity, but he mostly wanted to perk up the museum, bring it out of its spiritual and financial doldrums. The museum was languishing and needed a shot in the arm. He thought that a heist would give it a PR boost. He thought that the thieves would take the vase and a couple of paintings which no one can sell and leave. But they had their own agenda. They gave him the vase, which had no value to them, and kept everything else. Adler felt incredibly guilty to have caused the calamity out of stupidity. He's been desperately trying to get the art back, but the whole thing was out of his control."

"He was that naive?"

"Tizzio is still out there ready to accept order for art locked up in museums. I doubt anyone will unmask him."

Helen finds this amusing.

"The vase is as beautiful today as it was to me yesterday," Paris says. "Even knowing that it was made to order for Isabella. Its craftsmanship hasn't changed. What is art anyway? Objects or state of mind?"

They drink.

Paris says, "Oh yes. A photo. You and I will go on, grow older, but art preserves the instant and makes this moment eternal."

Paris puts his arm around Helen and turns her around so they both face the camera. Paris reaches over and flips the time delay lever on the camera.

"Smile."

They both hold up their glasses in festivity. His arm is

still around her. They release a big laugh, and it remains eternal, held forever by the image on the camera.

Helen puts down her drink. She cuts two slices of Velveeta and puts it on crackers. She gives one to Paris and raises her glass to toast.

"To art."

Made in the USA
Middletown, DE
28 September 2015